SURROUNDED

BY

USA TODAY BESTSELLING AUTHOR

MANDY HARBIN

Copyright © 2011, 2016, 2020 by Mandy Harbin

SURROUNDED BY PLEASURE
ISBN: 978-1-941467-51-0
ALL RIGHTS RESERVED

Cover Art by Letitia Hasser | RBA Designs

This book may not be reproduced or used in whole or in part by any existing means without written permission from Mandy Harbin, M.W. Muse, Penning Princess Publishing, or Mandolin Park, LLC.

This book is a work of fiction and any resemblance to persons, living or dead, or actual events is purely coincidental. The characters are products of the author's imagination and used fictitiously.

For more information, please join Mandy Harbin's Newsletter!

*To Dad for not reading some of my books,
but still gushing over how awesome I am.*

CHAPTER ONE

"Shit!" Krista Owens spilled her coffee on the transcript of the Lancaster deposition. She quickly scraped the offending liquid into her wastebasket and started wiping off the documentation. She so didn't need this.

Even though she'd been working at this firm for almost a year, she was still the newbie around here. The only reason she'd gotten this job fresh out of law school was because she'd interned here during the summer before starting her third year of schooling and had made an impression on the now junior partner—and newly married—Mikaela Woods.

As Krista wiped frantically at the paperwork and made a mental note to have her assistant make another copy before anyone found out, the sound of a throat clearing jolted her out of her musing. She popped up her head and locked her eyes on the very person she'd just been thinking about.

"Mikaela." *Great.* No covering up this little mess. She leaned back into her chair and guiltily held up the ruined document. For being a decent lawyer, Krista was such a horrible liar.

"That's coffee abuse, you know," Mikaela said with a smile as she entered the office and moved to sit down in front of Krista's desk.

Krista chuckled nervously. She liked Mikaela, but she was kind of like one of the bosses around here, and Krista felt as if she still had a lot to prove. The long hours and no days off? Yeah, they were getting to her. But she knew the score. She had to prove herself if she expected to make it. "I'm really sorry. I'll have Renee run off another copy."

"No reason to apologize to me. Now if you'd spilled *my* coffee, well, that'd be a different story."

Krista smiled and quickly tossed the file behind her onto her computer desk so that it was out of sight. And right atop a mountain of other work she'd yet to finish.

"How are things working out around here for you?"

Uh-oh. Krista's hands started shaking. Please don't fire me. Please don't fire me. Please don't fire me. "W-Why do you ask?"

"Well, I've been watching you, and you've been working on a lot of cases. How do you have any time for yourself?"

Krista laughed manically and then quickly stifled it. "Oh, I, um, I just take on what's assigned to me."

"So, Bill gave you all this work?" Mikaela shook her head. "I should've known," she mumbled, looking away. "That man is a tyrant." Then she took a deep breath and looked into Krista's eyes. "You need to learn to say no. It won't kill you." And then she laughed, which caused Krista to frown in a vain attempt to follow Mikaela's sudden mood changes. "And here I was going to ask if you wanted to help me out. Now I feel bad for not checking with you before talking to Bill."

"I'll help." She said it out of reflex, and Mikaela's eyes narrowed. Krista straightened in her seat. "I mean, what do you need help with?"

Mikaela sighed. "You know I've been working a lot from my husband's estate, right? I've got several cases I need finalized over the next month, but I also need to be in Texas to oversee the purchase of the adjacent acreage his family is purchasing from a competitor that's going out of business. The economy has been rough, but thankfully the Woods have invested well and are able to use this opportunity to expand their portfolio. I was going to see if you'd be interested in coming with me to help with my caseload while I orchestrate this purchase."

It was hard not to smile. Mikaela trusted her enough to ask her to help with her clients. This was an honor.

"You're the only one here that isn't married and could get away from home for a while without some spouse bitching," Mikaela continued.

Or maybe it wasn't an honor. She was just a pathetic loner. She never knew there'd be an award for being such a hermit. "I see."

"Oh, that came out wrong. Of course I

want your help, need your help. That's just what I told Bill to get him to agree to let you loose for about a month."

"Ah." She was so lame. Maybe if she got out more, she'd actually learn to have a life and not take things so seriously. But it was hard. Her parents had sheltered her to the point that her naïveté was sometimes painful. Sure, she was book-smart, but put her in a casual environment with strangers and she clammed up. It was no wonder she'd never had a boyfriend. Well, one that hadn't required batteries. Maybe if she was as pretty as Mikaela or as thin as her sister, Ariel, things would be different for her. But neither was the case. "Um, I'd love to help you, but I need to finish this before I can leave. When do you need me?"

"Krista." Mikaela's tone was reproach-ful, and Krista tried hard to keep the heat of embarrassment from creeping up her neck and into her face. "I'm going to have a little word with Bill about your caseload. And I think you should plan on coming with me to the Woods estate. Think of it as a vaca-tion. You'll still have to work, but knowing how hard you've been working your ass off here, it'd be like a month at a resort." She chuckled. "Only you'll be in the middle of the woods."

Woods she could do. And an almost vacation she could definitely do. This may be the only one she'd get for years because, regardless of what Mikaela thought about Krista's workload, she knew she still had to pay her dues and work the insane hours when she came back. "Sure. I'd love to come."

Mikaela stood, then smiled. "Good." She turned to leave but hesitated at the door, then looked over her shoulder. "One more thing. When you get down there, tell everyone you're in an open relationship."

Krista frowned. Open relationship? She'd have to be in one first. "Why?"

Mikaela's eyes got big, and she turned to face her fully, hand resting on the door-jamb. "Are you involved with someone?" Krista shook her head, and Mikaela looked as if she'd relaxed a little. Weird. "Let's just say my brothers-in-law are all very hot, but none of them will give you the time of day if you're single and clingy. Commitment issues." She shrugged. "If they think you're involved and happily in love but know your relationship is open sexually, you just might get lucky."

Why was her face suddenly blazing hot? Oh right, immediate humiliation would do that, wouldn't it? God, Krista had had no idea she looked that desperate. "I, um."

"Sweetie, I didn't mean..." Mikaela stepped closer to her, seemingly reading Krista's mortification. "I'm messing this up. I know we're not best friends, but we both practically live up here. Well, I do when I'm in town because I miss Josh, and you're always here. So I feel like we are friends, and I didn't mean to imply that you weren't capable of getting a man or to suggest that you even want one. I just think that since you'll be staying in the same house with three available men who happen to be smokin' hot it's my duty as a fellow woman to give you the lowdown on the situation. I know if I were in your shoes, I'd want a heads-up on something like that. It's easier to get lucky if you're prepared." Mikaela chuckled, then smiled softly. "Just give it some thought, okay? You only live once."

When she turned to leave, Krista stood and looked out the small office window and at the cloudy sky, not sure if it was clouds or smog she was trying to see through as she thought over Mikaela's parting words. Only living once? Yeah. Getting lucky? If only it were that easy.

———

TOBY WOODS HAULED scrap wood out of the thicket where the machinery wouldn't reach. Damn, but he was exhausted. They'd been clearing this section of their property where it bordered the Caldwell Tree Farm since their offer to purchase that land had been accepted. The guys were excited about expanding, even more so about the possibility of hiring permanent help. Right now, they hired seasonal help as needed, but with the addition of that land, they'd have to expand their operation. Plus, his dad was looking into retiring. Toby knew Josh was looking forward to working more in the office and less in the field, but Toby figured if they hired enough people, all the brothers could take office duties and decrease the manual labor part for all of them.

Because this shit was getting old.

Not that Toby had much of a choice. It wasn't like he could just waltz into town and fill out a job application at any ol' place. He envied those snotty-ass kids he'd come across online who bitched about their fast-food jobs. At least they got to meet new people.

And fuck.

Jesus, it'd been too long since he'd felt the warmth of a woman's thighs wrapped around his hips. He'd give anything to sink his hard cock into the depths of...

He groaned as he dropped the log he'd been dragging into the brush pile before trekking back into the woods, doing his best to keep the briars from snagging his face and trying to put his mind back on his job and off what he couldn't have. He needed to shift and run tonight. Maybe that'd help. He and his brothers hadn't shifted as often lately because Josh had been busy with his new wife, and Toby just hadn't felt like it. He knew he should've been happy for Josh that he'd found his mate—and deep down, he *was* happy for him—but he couldn't shake the feeling that he might never have what Josh now had. Toby figured his brothers felt the same way. Tonight, he'd run as a mountain lion, hunt, and maybe even sleep in the woods. Maybe if he embraced his feral side, he could shake this weird depression.

Toby and his brothers were mountain lion shifters. So were their parents. His father had changed their mother when they'd bonded all those years ago, and after she'd died a few years back, his dad hadn't found the need to take another mate. He could still be around available women without the overpowering need to take them just as if he were still mated. Josh was lucky things worked out with Mikaela when he'd taken her as his mate. Their youngest brother, Eric, hadn't fared so well.

At times Toby hated this life, but he knew there wasn't anything he could do about it. Knowledge was lacking since their father had been an orphan. Records had shown that Toby's grandparents were in an accident when his father, Thomas, was a toddler. For all they knew, they were the only ones of their kind in existence.

And if they weren't? Well, it wasn't like they could go walking around asking people if they turned into big cats with feral instincts to mate.

He heard the static on his radio before he heard Josh's voice. "Toby."

Sighing because he'd found himself feeling sorry for himself yet again, he brought the radio up to his mouth. "Yeah?"

"We're stopping early to meet in the den. You've got thirty minutes to shower and get there."

"Ten-four."

Toby holstered the radio and crept back out of the mass of limbs, briars, and trees, heading straight for his wheeler. Thirty minutes was just long enough to do a little washing and a little masturbating. Alone. Yeah, life sucked. Growling, he mounted the wheeler and hightailed it home, not stopping to talk to his dad, who'd been leaning against the pillar talking to Jeffery when he'd stalked by.

He rummaged around his room for a clean set of clothes, still feeling agitated, but as soon as he stepped into the shower, Toby immediately started to feel better. He wasn't sure if it was the relaxation of the hot water sluicing off his stiff muscles or the knowledge he'd be taking the edge off his growing need. But as he soaped up, lingering on his cock as the steam of the shower engulfed him, he didn't care what the reason was.

Bracing one hand on the tiled wall, he watched as he fisted the other over his erection. He knew just how to touch himself to end this quickly. No need to tease himself, prolonging his pleasure, because the gratification was shallow, meaningless. Oh, he needed it all right, but there was no use turning it into something it wasn't. As he tightened his grip and worked his cock harder, brutally stroking it, the ecstasy was climbing higher, faster. He threw his head back and groaned as lightning licked his balls and he shot his load all over the shower floor.

Panting, he slumped against the wall and angled the showerhead to rinse the evidence of his jacking off. Then he quickly washed again, got out, dried off, and dressed methodically. Everything was routine around here.

Everything.

Toby got up, ate breakfast with his family, worked in the field, took a lunch break, worked his ass off some more, showered, masturbated, shared drinks with his family, ate dinner, went to bed. Same damn thing every day. Nothing ever changed for him. When Mikaela had shown up here, he'd hoped for a change in the monotony. Well, he'd certainly gotten that wish. He should've been more specific. He'd wanted to bed her, but Josh had practically pissed all over her, marking her as his the moment she'd stepped foot on this estate.

Toby hadn't had a chance. None of his other brothers had either.

It was just as well, for Toby loved Mikaela, but not like Josh did. Those two were meant to be together. Toby figured that maybe when a man found his soul mate, he just knew.

At least he could hope.

As he neared the dining room, Toby heard some loud laughter and immediately smiled. That was Rob. He was always such a jokester, but lately he'd been in a funk, too. It was good to hear that sound coming from him again.

Toby opened the door, and his brothers looked at him. Jack was frowning; no shocker there. Jack was a sourpuss on his best day. Rob and Josh were smiling.

"What'd I miss?" he asked as he grabbed a glass for his scotch.

"Nada, brother," Josh said, chuckling. "Jack's just pissed he has to work in the Burnout Hole tomorrow."

"Fuck you, Josh."

"Not my type, man."

Rob choked on his drink as he tried not to laugh again, and Toby didn't even try to keep from chuckling.

The door swung up, and Toby turned to watch as his father joined them.

"Good evening, boys. I take it work was daunting as usual today."

The guys all grunted and nodded. Then Josh sat his drink down and faced everyone. "I've got some news that might cheer you up. Mikaela's bringing someone to help her with her lawyer stuff. She'll be staying here about a month or so while Mikaela helps us finalize the purchase of Caldwell's property."

"She?" Toby mumbled, and he was pretty sure he heard his brothers ask, too.

"Yes. Her name is Krista Owens. She's a young lawyer at Mikaela's firm."

Toby felt his hands tremble. He knew he shouldn't get his hopes up, but he couldn't stop his adrenaline from spiking.

"Dad and I have already talked about

this," Josh said, "and he's given the go-ahead for her to be here. She's not married—"

Toby gasped, which cut Josh off. Then he glanced over and saw Rob's jaw had dropped and Jack's eyes were narrowed.

"But she's taken. She's very much in love with a longtime boyfriend and plans to spend the rest of her life with him."

Toby's heart plummeted. He hadn't wanted to get his hopes up, but up they had been... right before crashing to the ground. Fuck, he couldn't catch a break. Not that he should've suspected anything differently. It was suicide to have an available woman around. His life sucked, but he had no intention of checking out early.

"Damn it, Josh," Jack growled. "Care to tell us how the fuck that's supposed to cheer us up? You want to dangle a woman in front of us for a month? One we can't have?"

"Dude, I think you're incapable of cheering up," Rob said, shaking his head at Jack, then turning to their dad and Josh. "But he has a point."

Josh smiled. "I said she was taken, not that she was off-limits."

Toby's head snapped up from the amber liquid he'd been studying. "Explain."

"Krista is in an open relationship. She loves her boyfriend, but they allow each other to fuck other people." Josh shrugged as if what he'd just said was the most un-complicated thing in the world, and Toby had to fight not to punch that grin off his face.

"What about Eric? Have you forgotten what happened to our brother? He'd gotten cozy fucking Pam while she was still mar-ried. She'd been in an open relationship when that started, too."

Josh frowned at him. "I know. I know this isn't perfect, but Eric hadn't known she'd gotten divorced either. You have nothing to worry about here."

Toby glanced at his dad, and he was just sitting back, quietly watching his sons argue.

"So, let me get this straight," Rob said as he stepped closer to Josh. "Are you ex-pecting us to take turns fucking her? Is she expecting that? 'Cause I gotta tell ya, I ain't into that shit."

"Oh, no. She's not expecting anything.

And nothing may happen with her. All I'm telling you is that if she chooses to pursue one of you, then I'm letting you know it's okay to fuck her."

"She's mine," Jack said as he took a sip of his scotch with an air of righteousness.

"Oh, fuck you, hotshot. You can't call dibs on pussy," Rob snarled.

"I'm the next to the oldest. It's my fucking turn." Jack took a step toward Rob, and Josh stepped between them, putting his hands on their chests.

"Listen, bro. It's up to her. It's okay if you want to pursue her, but you can't just claim her without giving the other guys a shot."

"What, like you did with Mikaela? You have such a fucking double standard." Jack shoved Josh's hand off his chest and stepped back.

"I hadn't tried staking a claim before even seeing her. Ms. Owens is a person, Jack, not a thing. You'd do well to remember that."

"Whatever." Jack waved his hand in dismissal. "I'm going after her."

"Me, too," Rob said.

They both looked at Toby. *Great.*

These two cats were acting like a couple of dogs fighting over a bone. Not only did he not want to get in the middle of his brothers, he just didn't want to risk it. Eric had been in a very similar situation before he'd died. Toby wanted no part of it.

"Thanks, but no thanks. You two can fight it out. I'm not chancing it."

And he wouldn't. He envied his life.

His pathetic life.

CHAPTER TWO

K RISTA STIFLED a yawn as she watched the countryside fly by. She'd already had a hard time picturing Mikaela living out in the country—the woman wore thousand-dollar shoes, for Christ's sake—but seeing her drive this testosterone machine beat all Krista had ever seen.

After pulling her glasses off, she rubbed the corners of her eyes, trying to revitalize them. She'd taken out her contacts to keep her eyes from drying out during the trip to the Woods estate, but sitting here with her glasses on, resting on a plush seat, she felt as if it were night-night time. With as much as she'd worked lately, sleep was a luxury.

If she forgot about the fact she'd stayed up half the night thinking about how crazy she was hoping some sexy man would whisk her off her feet and do naughty things to her, she didn't acknowledge that.

"How much farther do we have until we get there?"

Mikaela chuckled. "Oh, my God, if you start whining 'Are we there yet?' I'm going to reach across the seat and bonk you on the head."

"*Bonk you on the head?*" Krista laughed, and Mikaela laughed louder. As much as Krista tried putting Mikaela in a boss role, she could see her becoming a close friend. Not that Krista had many friends.

"For your information," Mikaela hesitated to turn on her blinker then pull up to a huge iron gate, "we're here."

"Oh, thank you, Jesus. I've had to pee for like the last twenty miles."

"Yeah, now you see why I had to stay here when I prepped that codicil for Mr. Woods. We left civilization about sixty miles ago." She rolled down the window and leaned out to punch in a bunch of numbers on the keypad. When she finished entering the code, she rolled up the window and waited for the gate to open.

"But there's a little town about ten or fifteen miles farther down the highway. No hotels, but there's a shitty little bar if you're so inclined." Mikaela smirked.

"I think not." She rarely went out with friends. No way was she venturing to an unfamiliar area by herself. Yeah, she was a grown-ass woman, but there were some things she just didn't do, and she had no interest in getting raped or killed while she dallied about all by her lonesome in a questionable establishment.

"Don't blame, ya. Maybe I can talk Josh into taking us out on the town one night."

Krista appreciated the offer but still had no desire to get all gussied up to be a third wheel. Instead of giving a definitive answer, she shrugged as she looked out the window. The driveway wasn't as narrow as she'd expected, considering the forest seemed to grow right up against it, but the picturesque ride through the curving path was truly breathtaking. The evergreen trees provided a canopy, sheltering them from the autumn sun. And as they entered a massive clearing, Krista gasped as she took in the huge log cabin. It looked like some custom mansion but was made to fit perfectly in its surroundings. Smaller cabins dotted the area, but even those buildings looked bigger than her apartment.

"I know. The house is beautiful," Mikaela said, seemingly reading Krista's thoughts.

"That's an understatement."

Mikaela parked, then Krista hopped out and started grabbing her bags. She would be staying a month, so she'd packed a lot. She seriously thought she had more with her now than what was left at her place.

"May I take your bags, ma'am?" a voice sounded behind her, and she whirled.

"Umm."

"This is Jeffery," Mikaela said, coming to her rescue. "He's, well, he's Thomas's everything. If you need anything, he'll get it for you. And if he can't, he'll find some way to make it happen anyway." She leaned over to hug Jeffery. He seemed a little startled by her action but returned the hug briefly before looking back at Krista.

"Ma'am?"

"Oh, yes, yes, of course. I mean, I can get some of them, but I wouldn't mind the help."

"That won't be necessary, ma'am. I'll have your bags in your room waiting for you by the time the lady of the house finishes with your tour."

"L-Lady of the house?" Hadn't Mikaela told her Mr. Woods was a widow?

"He means me." Mikaela shrugged like it was a silly notion, but she had a twinkle in her eyes that betrayed her nonchalance. "C'mon. Let me show you around before the guys finish up their work. I'm afraid once they lay their eyes on you they'll be monopolizing all your time. I think they're going to make it really difficult for me to get any real work out of you," she said, laughing as she motioned for Krista to follow her.

Oh, yeah, work. She couldn't forget the real reason she was here. Lots of hot monkey sex it was not.

———

"HOLY SHIT, DO YOU SMELL THAT?" Rob jumped off the limb he'd been perched on while the guys were taking a breather. "That's her. She's here." He inhaled again, groaning on his exhale.

Toby sniffed and immediately suppressed his own sound of pleasure. Rob was right. That smell was the sweetest thing he'd ever smelled in his life. And he'd smelled plenty of women in his past. Granted, they, too, were women already taken, but the smell of a ripe woman was still intoxicating.

This Krista chick had them all beat. She was ambrosia. And he was fucked. Truly fucked. He still didn't want to risk getting his ass handed to him by a pissed-off cougar lioness after being turned against her will, so he'd have to resist the temptation. And he would.

Jack stood suddenly. "I'm heading in to shower. See you in the dining room for drinks." Toby wanted to growl at... what? Jack had every right to prepare himself for meeting that woman. Toby should be happy Jack was so focused on getting in her panties. If his brother kept her distracted, maybe Toby would find it easy to resist her.

"Me, too." Rob hopped up and bolted without another word. *Fuck*. This sucked ass! No, no, this was a good thing. He sighed, looking down at his scuffed work boots.

"I'm heading in, too. I haven't seen Mikaela in two weeks." Josh leaned over and patted Toby's shoulder, then gave it a squeeze before turning and walking away.

Everyone had bailed, but technically the work was done for the day. Toby could do a few minuscule things, knowing he'd be stalling, or he could go shower, make nice with his pecker, and get ready for dinner.

He took a deep breath as he stood and almost fell to his knees when his legs started to buckle. God, that woman's scent would be the death of him.

Maybe he should jack off twice tonight. He walked off, but the closer he got to the house, the stronger her scent called to him.

Fuck. No maybe about it. His dick was hard as steel. Tonight he would be switching up the monotony with a twofer.

CHAPTER THREE

KRISTA PACED in her spacious bedroom, regretting the outfit she'd put on. She still had time to change out of the blue silk dress that complemented her eyes. The wrap style helped camouflage her rounded belly, but it made her boobs and butt look huge. The lacy bra and panties she'd run out and bought last week matched the color of the dress. She'd also purchased some additional matching sets to replace the holey granny panties and stretched-out flesh-tone bras she'd worn for years. She wanted to make a good impression and had all these great ideas of coming out of her shell with a bang.

Now she rather liked the idea of her

comfy, homey shell. This dress was too snug and just too revealing. She didn't feel sexy. She felt like an idiot, like a virgin playing dress-up. She wiped her sweaty palms along her arms as she looked at her opened closet door. She had time to change if she was quick about it. Hell, she'd spent the afternoon unpacking and organizing everything since she knew she was going to be here for a while. So she knew exactly where her favorite jeans were.

As she rushed over to the closet to grab them, she almost tripped over the pumps she had on. *Flats*. She'd change into flats, too. But a knock on her door stopped her.

The sound of Mikaela's voice had her groaning. "Don't you even think about changing out of that dress I helped you pick out."

"Go away." She walked to the closet and grabbed her jeans.

The doorknob jiggled, and then the door swung open.

"Not gonna happen, girl. And those jeans you're holding onto like a security blanket are staying off those sexy-ass legs of yours for the night."

Krista's heart raced. "M-Mikaela, I don't think I—"

"Damn, girl. I've seen you in court. You tear into top-notch attorneys without even batting an eye. This is just dinner with a group of down-to-earth men. They won't bite." Mikaela darted her eyes suspiciously, almost nervously, but she looked back so quickly that Krista didn't have time to fully analyze her behavior. "Unless you want them to." She shrugged with a smirk, then held out her hand. "C'mon. Since you're acting like this experience is a trip to the doctor's office, we'll treat the initial introductions like we're ripping off a bandage. That part will be over before you know it."

Mikaela's tone brooked no argument, so, on a sigh, Krista relented and walked toward her bossy colleague.

"Good girl." Mikaela shut the door and led the way to the dining hall.

I can do this, Krista chanted mentally. Mikaela's brothers-in-law were just men. It wasn't as if she'd never kissed a man before. She'd just never done much of anything else. *And you're never going to at this rate. Suck it up!* Okay, if she didn't find them attractive, then no harm in looking. If they were easy on the eyes, then no harm giving one of them a test run in between the sheets. Besides, she'd never see any of them again—not unless they were to come up to St. Louis for legal work, and that wasn't likely. As they neared a rustic-looking door with elegant iron work, Krista's stomach flipped. The voices coming from the other side of that door sounded deep, masculine. Sexy. Holy moly, she wasn't sure if she could do this. She wasn't some vixen out to snag a lay. She was a good girl.

She was a horny girl.

A virgin.

"You look constipated, hon'. Take a deep breath before I open this door. When we walk in, I'll get us some wine. Loosen you right up."

Krista nodded absently, mentally directing her lungs to inhale and exhale. When she blew out her breath, Mikaela opened the door, and she followed behind.

Good heavens! She stood wide-eyed, staring at all the hunks in the room. They all seemed to be about the same height, with varying shades of brown hair and tanned skin. The one wearing a green pull-over sweater walked over to Mikaela, eyes locked onto her like he was about to devour her. Had to be the hubby.

"Hi, kitten," he murmured, taking his wife into his arms and kissing her temple affectionately. Even though the action was simple, Krista felt the chemistry zinging around them and felt a little pang of sadness that she didn't have a man in her life who looked at her like that.

She'd have to get a man first.

He looked over at her and extended his hand. "You must be Krista. I'm Josh Woods. It's a pleasure."

She shook his hand, smiling. "Krista Owens. And you have a lovely home."

He nodded, pulling his hand away, leaving his other arm wrapped around his wife as he guided her toward the crowd. "Come. Let me introduce you to my family."

Krista followed, fighting the urge to stare at her pumps as they echoed from clicking on the hardwood floor.

"This is Rob, Jack, and Toby." He pointed to each of the men as he said their names, and they each stared at her intently. She wasn't sure if that was a good thing or a bad thing. Then the last dude looked away suddenly, and the one in the middle stepped forward, took her hand, and gave it a gentle shake as his thumb tenderly rubbed her skin.

"I'm Jackson Woods. Second to the oldest. And it's a pleasure to meet such a lovely, beautiful woman."

Wow. This guy was smooth. Where Josh had green eyes, this guy's were a deep blue, matching her own eye color. His hair was also cut short, shorter than this brothers'. She could see herself wrapping her legs around this hunk of man.

The one on the left stepped up and elbowed Jack to the side as Jack growled at the intrusion. She chuckled, and Jack glanced up at her, smiling tightly. *Hmm.* So his growl wasn't a playful sound. He really seemed irritated that his brother had stepped over. She wasn't sure how to feel about that. The guy was hot and all, but she didn't care much for pushy types.

How would you know? You'd have to mingle with men to know your type. Ugh, mental pep talks sucked, but the voice in her head was right. She couldn't write him off just yet.

"I'm Robert Woods. Rob. It's nice to meet you, Krista." He shook her hand with the same care Jack had shown her, but when he finished, instead of letting go, he held on, dropping their joined hands to his side. Weird, but okay. She could handle that. This guy was just as hot as Jack. His eyes were green, but where Josh's were a deep color, Rob's were a mossy green, almost hazel. "How do you like it here so far?"

"Um. I like it just fine. I just got here, though, so I might feel differently after a few weeks." She laughed, and he joined her, his eyes twinkling.

"Not if I have anything to do about it." He stepped closer, and she gasped, instinctively stepping away.

Mikaela stepped between them. "Take it down a notch, hotshot. I don't want her freaked out on her first day here."

Krista laughed nervously, tugging her hand free. Rob inclined his head, giving her a half smile as he stepped back.

"Toby?" Mikaela asked. The guy in question looked up from his drink, not looking at Krista at all.

"Yeah?"

"You going to come over here and introduce yourself?"

The guy hesitated, looking at Josh and then at Mikaela before taking the few steps necessary to stand before Krista. Only then did he look into her eyes again, and she got a better look at him. *Oh bejeezus*, his eyes were a blue-green mix, and when he gave her a tentative smile as if he were unsure how to act, he flashed a perfect set of dimples. She had a thing for dimples, and she immediately wondered if his very fine rear had them, too.

"Toby Woods. Just Toby. I'm the baby 'round here now." He quickly shook her hand, but before she had time to relish his touch, he let go, shoving his hand into his pocket and rocking on his heels. Toby let his eyes stray back over to Josh before he stepped away.

Unsure what to do now, Krista turned to Mikaela. "You said something about a drink."

Jack grabbed her elbow—gently but surely—and pulled her away from Mikaela, Josh, and Rob. "You can have whatever you want," he whispered in her ear as he led her to the table.

Okay, she might be a virgin, but she wasn't stupid. She knew Jack's response was innuendo, but she didn't quite know how to respond. "Er, wine?"

He pulled out a chair for her. "White or red, darlin'?"

"Red will be just fine."

"My kinda girl," Mikaela said as she came over and sat next to her. "Grab a bottle of merlot, Jack. We'll share."

"I'll get you a glass, kitten." Josh bent over and kissed Mikaela's cheek before striding out of the room. When the door opened, Krista could briefly see what looked like an expansive wine room, but her eyes went straight to Jack. He'd been pulling a bottle from the shelf but had turned, giving his brother an irritated look. The door swung shut before she could see much of anything else.

"Hello, gorgeous." Krista jumped at the voice coming from beside her and turned to look right at Rob. He'd taken the seat right next to her.

"Hi," she breathed. Okay, this was too weird. If she didn't know any better, she'd think these men were competing for her attention. *Ridiculous.* They were all tall, handsome, virile men. And she was a plain-Jane woman with a few extra pounds on her hips and no notches on her belt.

"I hope you like salmon. Jeffery is an excellent cook." He reached up and brushed a lock of hair behind her ear, his hand lingering on her cheek, his eyes boring into her.

"Yeah, I like salmon just fine." Unable to withstand the intensity of his stare—or his caress—she darted her eyes around the room. On her visual journey of avoidance, she saw Toby had taken a seat at the other end of the table. She was no social butterfly herself, but she figured he'd at least try to engage her more since she was the new one around here. However, when she saw the look on his face, that thought fled, and she had to stifle a gasp. He looked sad. So sad it almost seemed like longing or despair. But when their eyes met, he straightened in his seat as if he'd been slouching, which he hadn't been, cleared his throat, and gave her a courtesy nod before grabbing his drink and taking a sip.

She frowned as she watched him study his liquor as he'd done earlier during her initial introduction. Maybe he was just shy and not as forward as his brothers. She definitely couldn't fault him for that. She was so far out of her own comfort zone that she almost envied the reclusive brother with the sexy dimples. When Rob stroked her arm, she wished she were sitting next to Toby instead.

The door to the wine room swung open, startling her. Jack and Josh walked out, with Jack carrying a bottle of wine and Josh holding two glasses. They both walked to the table, but they had cold looks on their faces, and they both were staring at her. She trembled, not understanding the hatred, but as they stepped closer, she realized she wasn't the intended victim of their hateful gazes. They'd been staring at Rob. When she looked over at him, he was staring back at his brothers with the same narrowed expression on his face. What was their deal? And why was Rob holding onto her arm now?

"Umm—"

"Josh," Mikaela said quickly, and he immediately diverted his attention to his wife. His expression softened as he gave her a brief nod. Then he looked over at Jack and tugged at his arm as Krista pulled her arm free from Rob's grasp.

"C'mon, you can sit next to me." Josh took a seat next to the head of the table.

"Are you not going to sit next to your wife?" Krista asked incredulously. Why wouldn't he want to sit next to Mikaela?

Josh chuckled. "I figured she'd want to visit with you, and if I sat over there, I'd be too tempted to haul her away and make her eat dinner in bed." He looked at his wife and winked.

"Oh, you," she said, smiling. Then she looked at Krista. "See what I have to put up with around here? Nothing but a bunch of cavemen. It'll be nice to add some estrogen in the atmosphere."

"*Lumberjacks*, kitten. No cavemen around here."

Their banter seemed to calm the charged atmosphere, and Krista took a deep, settling breath.

The main door to the dining room suddenly opened and an older gentleman walked in. "I am terribly sorry I'm late." He walked right up to the head of the table and started to sit but caught Krista's eye and stood back up. "Sorry indeed. Where are my manners?" He walked over to her with his hand extended. "I'm Thomas Woods. You must be the lovely Krista Owens. Welcome to our home."

She stood, taking his hand. "Yes, sir. Nice to meet you."

"Likewise." He withdrew his hand and headed back to his seat at the head of the table, but he seemed agitated.

"How'd it go, Dad?" Josh asked as Jeffery walked in pushing a cart of food and started serving dinner.

"Not as well as I'd hoped. That damn," he glanced over at Krista, looking contrite, "forgive me." He then looked back at Josh. "That Pete Caldwell is a piece of work."

"Thomas, you weren't over there trying to negotiate the purchase, were you?" Mikaela asked.

"Sorry, dear, but Mr. Caldwell called me over under the pretense of showing boundary lines on the southern side of his property." Then he looked at each of his sons, saving Josh for last, and Krista figured he relied on that son more than the others when it came to business. "But actually, he told me his daughter is contesting the sale, so he's talking to his attorney about backing out of the deal."

"What?" Mikaela screeched. "Oh, hell no! You tell Mr. Caldwell that you two have already entered into a contract, and that—never mind." She waved her hand dismissively. "*I'll* talk to his attorney. Don't you worry one bit, Thomas. I'll get this cleared up."

Thomas looked at Mikaela, and Krista could see that when he exhaled, a weight had been lifted off his shoulders. "Thank you, dear. I wasn't sure what to tell him when he blindsided me with that."

Without even thinking about it, Krista opened her mouth. "If Caldwell's daughter contests the sale and she has a legitimate claim to the property, it will prolong the closing." *If the Woods are even successful with the purchase now,* but she didn't say that.

Mikaela looked at her, and she could feel her cheeks heating. Maybe she should've just kept her mouth closed. She was here to help Mikaela with her other workload. Not this land purchase.

"I know. But she'd have to prove she

has a stake in the property for her claim to be valid."

"There could be any number of valid claims she could make. If he's incorporated and she's a major stockholder or board member, if his holdings are in a trust and she's the beneficiary, heck, even if she stands up and says her father is not in his right mind and can produce a power of attorney, anything can prolong or invalidate the sale."

"His holdings are not in a trust. He is incorporated, but she wasn't on the board of directors, but surely she's one of his heirs."

"Not that I don't like watching two gorgeous women flex their brainpower, but what does it all boil down to?" Rob asked, then reached over and caressed Krista's knee. She tried not to jerk away at the sudden contact. Again.

"It means," Mikaela started, "this purchase could take much longer than I was planning on."

Krista could read the real answer in Mikaela's eyes. She was going to be here longer than a month. Stuck. With one man who couldn't keep his hands off her, another who looked ready to pummel said touchy-feely brother, and another who acted like her very existence here was a major hindrance.

Great.

So, why did Mikaela look almost relieved?

CHAPTER FOUR

Toby kept his nose down, studying his drink. He was going to start eating as soon as Jeffery put his plate down in front of him because he was starving and the sooner he ate, the sooner he could get out of here. But as he stared at his salmon and asparagus, salivating, he just couldn't seem to pick up his fork and eat. It physically pained him to try to eat, and he immediately thought about how his father had always waited for his mother to take the first bite before he'd dive in at any meal. And Josh acted the same way with Mikaela. Hell, he'd started that shit from the first day he met her. Unable to help himself, Toby glanced at his sister-in-law as he remembered. But his eyes immediately darted to Krista.

God, she was fucking beautiful. A head full of billowy brown hair and eyes the color of the sky. And her body? He'd never envisioned a woman so luscious with curves in all the right places. His dick twitched at the sight of her ample cleavage. And her smell was downright intoxicating and went straight to his balls. His whole body tightened when she walked into the room in that killer dress. And when she opened up her mouth to speak, tingles shot down his spine. But his reaction tonight wasn't totally physical. Listening to his brothers fight over her was making something very primal rise up in him. Too damn bad, though. He was not, was *not* going to get in the middle of that. She was an incredibly sexy woman with an air of innocence about her, but Toby was not going to risk his life. Or hers. Even if he felt something for her—which he didn't, *damn it*— he'd be doing her a favor by not giving her more attention to deflect. His brothers were doing enough already. And it was pissing him off.

When Jack and Josh had walked out of the wine room, everyone within a five-mile radius and the ability to hear mental communication would've heard Jack's mental roaring and cussing at Rob for getting close to Krista and touching her. It took everything Toby had not to snarl at Jack and Rob and inform them... what? He wasn't even going to go there. It didn't matter what he thought in the heat of the moment. Krista Owens was off-limits to him.

So, why couldn't he pick up his damn fork and eat?

You know why.

Fuck. He wasn't going to entertain the idea of Krista being his mate. Even if he wanted to fuck her—okay, so he wanted to fuck her. He wasn't crazy, but even if he was going to pursue the opportunity to fuck her, it wasn't as if he could mate with her. She was in a loving, committed relationship. So, the whole can't-eat-before-my-female-does mentality shouldn't apply. There was no way she could ever be his in the lifetime bonding sense.

The crushing weight of sadness that thought brought on would just have to be ignored. And apparently, he would have to ignore it for longer than a month if what the ladies were arguing about the purchase of the Caldwell land was true.

Renewing his effort, Toby stared at his fork and slowly reached for it. Feeling sweat pop up on his brow, he refused to look up. He was a fucking adult, an *unmated* adult, who could eat whenever he damn well pleased. As he grasped his fork, he felt a surge of victory, and when he dug in, scooping a piece of salmon and shoving it into his mouth, he couldn't help feeling like a giddy kid. He was eating, which meant those silly thoughts about Krista and mating where just overreaction. He chewed, smiling, as he glanced up at everybody else, unable to hide the relief on his face.

Sonofabitch! She was already eating.

He fought the very childish need to drop his fork and storm out without eating. If he weren't so fucking hungry, he'd totally do that.

You okay, man? Toby's head snapped up at Josh's mental question. It wasn't like Toby could tell him what was on his mind. Everyone in this room with the ability to shift into a mountain lion would be able to hear their conversation just as if they were talking aloud. But Toby knew that he'd still keep his thoughts to himself even if only Josh could hear the conversation.

Yeah, bro. I'm good.

You don't look it. You'd better keep your ass over on that side of the table. I have enough shit to deal with since Rob's touching my woman. I won't tolerate you doing it, too, Jack warned.

Dude, she ain't yours, Rob said as his hand moved under the table, obviously touching Krista some more. *She's mine as long as she's here.*

It took all Toby's willpower not to growl out loud, much less through their mental communication. Jack wasn't as con-trolled, as the animalistic sounds vibrated through their connection.

Enough! I will not have my sons fighting over her like she's prey. You will show her respect and allow her to make the choice. Now enough with the mental com-munication with Krista around. She's a smart woman, and I don't want her getting suspicious.

Toby looked away and went back to his meal. Getting reamed by his dad wasn't on the top of his list of the most enjoyable activities. So, he'd just keep his focus on his food and get the hell out of here.

Toby was almost finished eating when he caught Mikaela and Krista whispering. He didn't want to keep looking, but the distressed look on Krista's face had his protective instincts flaring without warning. Then Mikaela stood, followed by Josh.

"We're going to bed. Goodnight, everyone." Mikaela smiled.

Fearing he'd be stuck here with Krista, Toby shot up. "I'm going—"

"Me, too," Krista said at the same time, standing when he did. They both stared at each other, and Toby knew the shock he saw on Krista's face mirrored his own. Mikaela, on the other hand, was grinning like a shit-eating possum.

"Oh, perfect. Toby, can you see Krista to her room? We'd do it, but you know we stay in one of the cabins now."

"Er." What the fuck was he supposed to say? Krista knew where her room was. As far as he knew, she'd already unpacked and showered. Naked. In the shower, all soaped up, rubbing her body, caressing her breasts. *Whoa*. Must avoid all thoughts of her in the shower.

"I'll do it," Jack stood.

"You haven't finished eating. Sit down," Thomas said, frowning.

"Then I'll do it," Rob said after swallowing the biggest bite of food Toby had ever seen him eat.

"Don't be silly. Toby was just leaving anyway. Isn't that right, son?"

Shit. Just what he needed. Another reproving look from his father. Okay, he could do this. He needed to get used to her being around anyway. If he went out of his way to avoid her at all cost, then his father would know something was up. Not that he cared if everyone knew he didn't want to pursue Krista sexually, but if his dad thought he was being rude to her, it'd backfire. And he didn't want to spend hours talking to his dad about Krista and engaging in more activities with her in an effort to make her feel welcome. He needed to keep his interaction with her to a minimum without overdoing it.

Throwing on a smile, he looked over at Krista. "Of course. I'd be happy to escort you."

Then she smiled back, and he knew he was totally fucked.

———

KRISTA FELT weak staring at those killer dimples. *Gawd,* she was a mess. She'd just wanted to get away from the man pawing at her and the other one staring at her so hard it was as if he were trying to coax her over to him through sheer will alone. She didn't even know how to feel about the sexy silent one. She felt like Goldilocks trying out the three bears. One brother was just too intense, the other was too forward, and the other didn't seem to want anything to do with her. Of course that one was the one who seemed to get her engine running. Maybe it was her sense of self-preservation that drew her to him. There was no doubt in her mind if she invited one of the other two up to her room, he'd take her up on the offer. But for some reason, she felt safe with Toby. Like she didn't have to anticipate where his unwanted hands would land or worry if he'd burn holes in her with his unnerving stare. Even though he didn't seem too thrilled with her, she was relieved it was him and not one of his brothers walking her to her room.

"Thanks," she breathed, stepping away from the table.

He walked around and joined her. But as they walked out of the dining room, Krista could see how rigid his shoulders were. He didn't engage her in conversation as they walked down the hall, solidifying her theory that he didn't want anything to do with her. After experiencing the unwanted attention from his brothers, Krista knew Toby's behavior should've been flattering.

She was quickly finding out that it was not.

She was attracted to this man, but he didn't seem to reciprocate. Maybe she should just bite the bullet and make the first move. Just the thought of coming on to him made her feel queasy. She was not some temptress. If she made a pass, she'd probably just make a fool of herself instead.

But she wasn't getting any younger, and all the thoughts she had before coming out here—thoughts of finally having wild monkey sex, or just having sex, period—flooded her mind. So what if she made a fool of herself? She'd never see Toby again. And if she were desperate enough to lose her virginity down here, she could always tap one of his brothers. An involuntary shiver attacked her with that ugly thought. It seemed that as soon as she looked at Toby, no other man would do. Okay, she wasn't going to think too much on that! But she needed to get this man talking if anything was ever going to happen.

"H-How do you like working with your family?" *Lame-o question. But too late to retract it.*

"I like it just fine. Nothing special. I hope with the purchase of the Caldwell Tree Farm we can get more permanent help to do the labor-intensive stuff and me and my brothers can take on more of the business aspect of the operation."

He sounded so sexy, too. And, oh Lord, his smell was something right out of a woodsman catalogue. Her hands trembled being this close to such a strong, virile man. "That'd be good. I mean being able to do more work in the office. What kind of cologne are you wearing?" she blurted out and then stifled a groan at her awkward behavior.

He paused, and she looked up at him.

All the way up into those gorgeous blue-green eyes. "Um, I'm not wearing any."

"Then why do you smell so good?" She covered her mouth on a gasp. What the hell was wrong with her? She was so not good at subtle flirting. Maybe next she should just throw her dress over her head and ask him to play with her pee-pee. *Lord have mercy.* At least they were standing outside her room, so she could run and hide now.

He chuckled, leaning into her space, and all thoughts of awkwardness fled, being replaced with very naughty ones. What was it about this man that made her heart go pitter-patter? She looked away, trying to rein in her raging hormones. But when she felt something against her hair and heard a soft moan, she yanked her head back in Toby's direction just in time to see him lean away, rubbing his mouth with the back of his hand. His eyes were a mixture of melt-her-panties heat and mortification. Confused, she reached up and touched her hair, feeling a slight dampness at the spot.

"Did you... Did you just lick my hair?"

He slowly shook his head, keeping his eyes on her as he moved his hand away from his face. "It was standing up, so I smoothed it down. My hands are just sweating."

The thought of him fixing her hair gave her a tingling feeling in the pit of her stomach. Why, she didn't know. It was such a small thing, but he did it for her. And the confession about his hands sweating only comforted her because it meant he was nervous, too, and he didn't mind telling her he was. He made her feel comfortable.

He made her horny.

Knowing she'd regret it if she didn't do something, she stepped forward and brought her hands up to his cheeks, stroking his face gently. "My hands are sweating too, see?"

He grabbed her wrists, and she thought he was going to push her away. But he just stood there, his eyes searching hers almost frantically. Then with a groan he released her wrists, buried his hands in her hair, and crushed his lips to hers, kissing her with a sense of desperation she didn't quite understand but didn't bother trying to figure out. All that mattered was he was kissing her and he tasted even better than he smelled. His tongue licked her seam, and she was all too eager to open up for him. The feel of his tongue rubbing against hers was her downfall. Her knees buckled, but one of his arms shot around her back and grasped her waist, which kept her upright, as his other hand stayed in her hair to hold her head for his assault on her mouth.

She moaned, unable to process all the emotions roaring through her, and that needy sound seemed to fuel him on. He backed her against the wall by her bedroom door, and he fumbled with the knob. Once he got it open, he lifted her like she didn't weigh anything and carried her into the room while never stopping his kiss. He kicked the door shut as her feet found the floor again, only to find herself being backed up against the side wall.

He softened his kiss, his mouth sipping at hers as his hands landed on her hips, caressing her, gentling her, and she felt her pussy flood with her juices. God, she was ready for this. All these years not thinking about when she'd ever have sex, and now she couldn't wait. Because it finally felt right. She wound her arms around his neck and fisted her hands in his hair. Kissing him back with as much passion as he was kissing her. Then his lips left hers, and he kissed, licked, and nipped his way down her throat. Her hips thrust forward of their own volition, and she came in contact with his hard cock. Gasping, she couldn't help but want more, so she reached down and grabbed him through his slacks.

He groaned, thrusting into her touch. "Fuck, Krista, you don't know what you're doing to me." He grabbed the sleeve of her dress and tugged, pulling it along with her bra strap, exposing her breast. "Sweet Jesus." He swooped down, sucking her nipple into his mouth.

She moaned, her head falling back as he feasted on her breast while tugging her dress on the other side, releasing her other breast. As he kissed, nipped, and licked one nipple, he pinched, tugged, and rolled the other one with his fingers.

Krista had never felt something this intense, feeling Toby's mouth and hands on her, listening to his grunts and groans as he gorged on her body.

She released his cock and heard him whimper, but she wasn't planning on neglecting him for long. *Oh, no.* She wanted skin on skin. She yanked on his belt as he switched his mouth to her other breast. She gasped as she felt the air hit her wet, sensitive nipple and then moaned as his fingers raked over it gently while his mouth ravished her other one.

After she unfastened his belt, she unbuttoned his pants and drew down his zipper, the rasp of it one of the sexiest sounds she thought she'd ever heard before. Until the guttural groan that escaped Toby when she wrapped her hand around his pulsing cock. *That* was the sexist sound she'd ever heard in her life! Knowing she was giving a man this kind of pleasure before sex was one hell of an ego boost. She stroked him, using his leaking moisture to slicken her movements, but as she worked his cock, her pussy was clenching on nothing, aching to be penetrated. She rocked her hips back and forth, seeking contact, and he didn't disappoint. When his mouth left her breast and found her lips, his leg shoved between hers, and she gasped into his mouth as she rode his thigh.

"That's it, baby," Toby murmured against her lips. He was gathering her dress up with both hands, and with sudden nervous energy, she squeezed his dick and pumped him faster. He grabbed her wrist, stilling her. "Slow down, little vixen. I don't wanna come yet."

Her heart was pounding and her body trembling as his finger slid under the edge of her panties. He found her wet and ready for him.

"Fuck, fuck, Krista. You're so fucking wet, baby," he groaned, kissing along her neck, and thrust his dick into her hand. She started stroking him again as she gasped at his intimate touch. So good, so damn good. But with her heart going a mile a minute, she frantically wondered if she should say something to him about her inexperience. As he rubbed around her clit and slid down to her opening, she couldn't help but squeak as he gently prodded her entrance.

"I'm a virgin," she blurted out nervously.

He instantly stilled, panting on her neck. Then he leaned back and looked into her eyes. "What?"

Heat suffused her cheeks. "I-I said, I'm a virgin," she whispered, unable to find her voice.

He swore then pulled his hand out of her panties, so she automatically let go of his cock. Not looking at her face, he gently pulled her dress and bra back up, covering her. Then he stepped back, swallowing convulsively, and tucked his dick back in before zipping up and buckling his belt.

Finally, he looked at her as he took another step back. "I'm sorry. I shouldn't have gotten carried away like that. Please forgive me."

Too stunned to say anything, she just watched as Toby turned and left her room.

CHAPTER FIVE

Smooth move. That was all Krista thought about as she'd tossed and turned last night, then throughout her shower and late breakfast this morning, and now sitting in the office she'd be sharing with Mikaela for the next month at least. Blurting out her virginity status during the height of passion was a rookie mistake. She should've just suppressed her nerves and allowed Toby to pleasure her without any kind of disclosure. It wasn't like she still had her hymen, so he wouldn't have had to experience breaking through her barrier. No, she'd had to turn to taking care of herself over the years, so that little piece of tissue had long been obliterated thanks to the wonders of modern sexual technology and the glorious privacy of the Internet.

Trying to focus on the task at hand, Krista flipped through case files and organized them into various piles, identifying ones that could be quickly resolved and others that needed immediate action taken because those required long waiting periods for the other parties to file responses within their statutory time frames. She'd work on those cases first. The other, less-pressing ones could be handled later.

As she shuffled through the documentation, reading and preparing the appropriate motions, answers, and other pleadings, she did her best not to think about one tall, tanned, brown-haired, and blue-green–eyed hottie who gave her more pleasure in those short, few minutes last night than any man had ever given her. Hell, even more pleasure than she'd ever given herself, and she hadn't even climaxed! Toby's deft hands were calloused but tender, and his kiss... oh, Lord, could that man kiss! He tasted of whiskey and raw sexual desire. His tongue had done things to her mouth, her *breasts* that sent jolts of need right to her core. She'd love nothing more than to pull her panties down and shove his face right between—

"Good morning, girl. Sorry I'm running a little late," Mikaela said as she came barreling through the office door, clutching a cup of coffee. "Why is your skin all red? Are you hot? I can adjust the thermostat if you want." But she gave her a knowing look, and Krista felt herself blushing harder.

Oh, great. She probably looked like she'd rather be getting laid when she should be focused on her work. No more thoughts of Toby and his tongue! Krista shook her head and gave Mikaela a tight smile. "No, I'm fine. Just trying to weed through these cases."

It didn't look like Mikaela bought her answer, but to Krista's relief, Mikaela sat down and started explaining her calendar and what needed the most attention. Krista was pleased when Mikaela praised her after realizing she'd already identified the more-pressing work and had started on those. Then they'd spent several hours working—Krista on Mikaela's existing caseload and Mikaela on the phone with the Caldwells' attorney, getting answers on the news Thomas had shared last night. Krista got so into her work groove she'd figured Mikaela had forgotten about the look on Krista's face when she came into the office this morning.

"So, how'd it go with Toby last night?"

Krista jerked her head up to see Mikaela casually looking over some paperwork.

"Fine." Crap, why did her voice have to crack? And now Mikaela was looking at her.

"Really?" Mikaela smirked. "What happened?"

"Nothing." Another squeak of a response.

"Hmm. I don't believe you, counselor. Let the record show you were flushed when I came in this morning, and Toby was even more evasive this morning at breakfast than you're being now."

"Don't you 'counselor' me, counselor. And enough with the interrogation business. I'm not talking about it." *Oh, God.* Mikaela saw Toby this morning at breakfast. Krista wanted to see him, but then again, she wanted to avoid him. She was insanely attracted to him, yet totally embarrassed by the idea of having to face him again. She knew she wouldn't be able to avoid him forever, but if she buried herself in her work, she didn't have to think about what she should do about him.

Mikaela sighed, moving closer to her. "Listen. I just want to help. He seemed to really like you, and—"

"They all did," Krista muttered, watching her hands as they twisted together.

Mikaela chuckled. "Yes, well, they're men and you're beautiful. Of course they're interested in you, but Toby seemed to have genuine interest going on." She leaned closer, whispering, "And I think you reciprocate that interest."

"Yeah." What else could she say? There was no use denying the fact Toby was a hottie. "But I messed up." Big time.

"So, what happened?"

Krista groaned and looked up at her. "He, er, kissed me. A lot. We were in my room, making out, and I, I, *shit*." She shook her head. "I blurted out I'm a virgin, and he wigged out and bolted. There. Are you happy now? I'm a total idiot." She slumped back in her chair and covered her face, hoping to shield her humiliation.

"You never said you were a virgin," Mikaela said woodenly.

Krista's hands slid down her face. "That's not something I go bragging about. Granted, I don't think there's any shame in it. The right guy just hasn't come along, not that I've been waiting around for Mr. Right. I've just been too busy to go fishing in the sea of bodily lust." Then why did being in Toby's arms feel so incredibly right, as if she'd been saving herself for him all along? Ridiculous. That was what that was.

Mikaela seemed lost in her thoughts, so Krista didn't continue. Then Mikaela looked over at her with an odd expression. "They'll never believe you're in a loving relationship that's open sexually if you've never had sex before. What boyfriend in his right mind would not have sex with you but allow you to have sex with other men?"

"I don't have a boyfriend, remember?" But even as Krista said it, she realized that Mikaela was really talking to herself and not to Krista. "Hey? What's the big deal?"

Mikaela blinked as if she'd snapped out

of whatever trance she was in and looked at Krista, finally seeing her. "Huh?"

"I said what's the big deal about the guys knowing I'm not in a relationship?" Hell, if what Mikaela said was true and they shy away from commitment, then maybe Jack and Rob would back off if they knew she was actually available. Maybe finding out she wasn't really a challenge by being in a relationship or some kind of loose woman who'd fuck anything that moved because of an unorthodox relationship they'd just leave her alone.

Seemed to have worked for Toby. As soon as she'd told him she was a virgin, he'd lost interest immediately. A heavy feeling settled in her chest, and she didn't understand why. *Unless that's what real rejection feels like.*

"No. No." Mikaela stood, stalking around the room. "Let me think."

What in the world was there to think about? Krista had only been here a day and had already screwed up any chance she had at finally discovering what sex with a living penis felt like.

After several minutes of Mikaela pacing the room, she finally turned. "I got it. Just tell Toby you don't want anybody else knowing about your virginity. That it's a personal thing and you don't want everyone knowing about your personal life."

"Even though I like that idea very much," Krista began, because she definitely didn't want people talking about her sex life, "how does that help, exactly? Not that I want Toby to believe I'm in a relationship, but you said it yourself. No man will not have sex with his girlfriend if they're in an open relationship." She rubbed her head and looked away. "Besides, I don't think he really cares anymore."

Mikaela came over and sat next to her. "I think you're wrong. If I know Toby, he stopped because he *does* care. At least about not taking advantage of you." She patted Krista's knee. "We just need to convince him to keep quiet about the news, and you need to show him you're sure about taking this step with him."

"I was already out of my comfort zone last night when we, er, last night," she finished lamely. "I'm not sure how to convince him that it's him I want."

Mikaela clutched Krista's shoulder.

"Answer me this one question. Is it Toby that you truly want? I mean, I figured you wanted him over the other two guys, and I admit I wanted you to cut loose while you were here and have some fun. But I didn't know you were a virgin. So, when I ask if it's Toby you want, I mean would you still pick him if you were at some random bar and he was there with a hundred other guys all vying for your attention, or is it a case of getting the pick of the litter, so to speak?"

Krista chuckled at Mikaela's terminology, but then sobered as she considered her answer. She knew she was here on business, but she also understood there'd be men around. She did pack accordingly, bringing the new lacy underclothes and whatnots, hoping she'd get laid. But the truth was she was attracted to Toby, and she didn't see that attraction being a product of convenience. "Yeah," she finally answered. "Yeah, I think I'd still pick him out of a crowded room. There's just something about him. I can't explain it, but I want to get to know him, and I want him to be my first. I'm just at a loss of what to do now."

Mikaela smiled. "Don't you worry about that. If it's Toby you want, then it's Toby you'll get. As of tonight, you'll let your preference be known to all the guys, and Toby will not be able to resist you."

Dubiously, Krista asked, "How so? What am I doing tonight?"

"*We're* crashing the guys' poker game with a little game-playing of our own."

Trying to soak up some of Mikaela's enthusiasm, Krista hoped the gamble would pay off.

———

TOBY SAT in the den around the card table with his brothers, nursing his beer and fighting the urge to get something stronger to drown his sorrows. Last night had been magic, electrifying, and over way too soon. He wanted Krista as much as he needed his next breath. He knew it'd been years since he'd been with a woman, so he tried to blame his insistent need for her on that. But it just felt like an excuse. He'd long ago grown accustomed to not having sex with the occasional taken woman after his brother died. The way he saw it, he was nearing thirty and had experienced enough casual sex to last him a lifetime.

Or so he'd felt before touching Krista. When she'd put her fingers on his cheeks, she'd ignited an urgency inside him to take her. He wanted nothing more in that moment than to sink inside her welcoming heat and pound into her throughout the night, over and over, until neither of them could move. Hell, her touch had been just an innocent caress because the only reason she'd put her hands on his face was because she was trying to comfort him about his sweaty hands comment.

And his hands had been sweaty, but it hadn't been his hands on her hair last night, either. She'd called him out on him licking her hair. Just like he couldn't eat before her last night, when he'd seen her hair slightly disheveled, he instinctively tried to groom her.

Just like the fucking cat I am.

As soon as he'd touched her hair with his tongue, he knew his mistake, but there'd been no going back. He'd just been grateful his nerves had provided a valid excuse, leading to more intimate touches.

And he'd have fucked her all night long

if she hadn't told him she was a virgin. *Jesus!* He'd never had sex with a virgin. Hearing her say those words should've been like dousing ice water on his dick, but instead all he could think was *mine*. It'd taken a monumental effort to turn away from her last night, but he'd done it. He respected her too much to take something as precious as that from her.

No matter how much he wanted to be the one to do it.

No matter how much he wanted to be the only one to ever have sex with her ever again.

"Deuces wild," Jack muttered as he dealt the next hand.

"Still not talking about last night, eh?" Rob asked as he shoved his cards into his hands.

"Nothing to tell." Toby shrugged, organizing his own cards. Whatever happened —or didn't happen—last night was nobody's business as far as he was concerned.

"You had your chance and struck out," Rob said as he threw some chips into the pot, raising the bid. "I'm sure I'll have better luck."

Josh matched Rob's bid, and Jack

folded. After Toby raised again, Rob called. Josh won, and the other guys tossed their cards into a pile.

"Not if I get to her first," Jack growled, taking a swig of his beer.

"You both need to just back off and give her some damn breathing room," Toby barked as Rob dealt the next hand.

Josh smiled at him as he took a pull on his beer, thankfully not voicing anything.

"Oh, no, brother, you didn't do any backing off last night," Jack said. "You got lucky getting the opportunity to take her to her room, and it's not our fault you weren't able to charm the panties off her."

Toby growled and slammed his beer down, holding it in a death grip. He was about to come across this table and punch the daylights out of his older brother when the door to the den swung open and Mikaela and Krista walked in.

Toby stood, as did his brothers, since it was the polite thing to do, but the moment his eyes landed on Krista, he couldn't look away.

Oh, God. She was wearing jeans and cowboy boots and an unbuttoned flannel shirt exposing a white tank top. A sexy, little, low-cut, white tank top. *Shit.* His dick was getting hard just staring at how incredibly hot her curvy body was, showcased in such casual clothing.

Mikaela fanned her hands. "Sit, sit. We just got bored hanging out by ourselves and figured we'd see what you guys were up to."

The guys all sat. Toby immediately grabbed his beer and took a long drink.

"Hi, kitten. Did you get a lot of work done today?" Josh asked Mikaela as the girls got closer to the table.

Mikaela sat on Josh's lap and kissed him. "Mmm-hmm."

But Toby wasn't paying attention to his brother and his brother's wife. His eyes were glued on the hot goddess sashaying around the table.

And she was staring right back at him.

Fuck, she was coming closer.

Then to his utter shock, she sat on his lap. *Holy shit!* He gaped at her as she took the beer out of his hand and guzzled it, her pale throat working as she swallowed it down. Reflexively, he put his arm around her to steady her on his lap, but he was unable to take his eyes off the smooth column of her neck. He couldn't help it—he groaned and leaned closer to her, smelling her freshly washed skin. Finally she pulled the bottle away from her luscious mouth and turned to him, licking the rim.

"Yummy. Tastes like you."

What the fuck! I thought you said nothing happened last night, Rob yelled mentally.

But Toby didn't acknowledge him. All he could do was watch his little vixen lick that bottle like she was relishing the taste of his cock. His already hard dick grew impossibly harder.

"Is that right?" Toby murmured.

"Oh, yeah." After one last lick, she handed the beer back to him. "You should see if it tastes like me now."

Keeping his eyes on her, he brought the bottle up to his lips and licked before taking a swig. Krista nuzzled his neck and brought her lips up to his ear. "I love the way you taste," she whispered.

Oh, fuck it. He could do a whole hell of a lot of things with this woman that didn't actually include penetration. Starting with the both of them tasting each other all over. As he put the beer on the table, he leaned in for a kiss. The beer bottle did have a faint flavor of her, but he wanted it directly from the source.

But as he got near to her lips, she turned and picked up his cards. "Can I play with you?"

"You can play with me anytime, baby." He pulled her closer to him, her thigh rubbing against his erection. Her gaze cut to him, and a knowing smile teased her lips. She pressed her leg harder against his cock, and his mouth fell open on a soft growl.

"It's your bet, hotshot," Jack snapped.

Toby sat a little straighter, pulling the cards Krista was holding into view. "What do you think?" he asked her.

"Hmm. I don't know. I think we should raise."

"You don't even know what the current bet is," Rob grumbled.

Toby's head snapped at Rob. *Knock it off!* He picked up a couple of chips and then a few more. "Doesn't matter. We're raising."

Everyone looked over at Josh for his bet, but he was too busy kissing his wife. Toby tried to hide his smile but was unsuccessful. "Josh, dude, it's your turn, man."

He pulled away from Mikaela's mouth

and looked at his cards, but he didn't seem to be paying much attention since his wife was kissing his neck and rubbing his chest. "Call." He threw a bunch of chips into the pile then slid his hand into his wife's hair, pulling her mouth back to his.

Toby chuckled at his brother's public display of affection, but his laughter died when he felt Krista's tongue in his ear. He groaned, fisting a hand in her hair to hold her close, keeping her mouth right where he wanted it.

At least for now. Later he'd want her mouth other places. His dick twitched, seconding that mental suggestion.

"Pair of aces," Jack grumbled, tossing his cards over.

"Two pair. Jacks high," Rob said curtly, showing his cards.

"Full house," Toby panted, flipping his cards over then wrapping that arm around Krista's waist.

"Beats me," Josh said.

"Fuck, can you two jackasses pay attention for one damn minute?" Jack said.

Krista pulled away, wiping her lips. She looked at the other guys, but Toby couldn't take his eyes off her.

"Sorry," she said sweetly. "I'll behave. I swear."

"Yeah, yeah. Me, too," Mikaela agreed.

"It's my turn to deal," Jack said, reaching for the deck and gathering the cards everyone tossed over to him.

Toby turned his head and nuzzled Krista's neck. "I take it you're not mad at me for leaving last night?" he whispered.

She turned to look at him, stroking his cheek. "Not at all," she said, matching his tone. "I think it was a very noble thing you did." She quirked an eyebrow. "Unnecessary, but noble."

He chuckled softly, then gave her a quick kiss, knowing if he lingered, he'd maul her right here at this table.

"Um, I'd like to keep what was said just between us," she murmured. "You know... about me."

He stroked her cheek then rested his forehead against hers. "Of course. But, er, I think we have some things to clear up." Like how the hell her boyfriend agreed to her having an open relationship when that guy hadn't even fucked her. That thought hadn't escaped him. In fact, it'd been the thought dominating all others since he'd left her last night. He couldn't find a reason that made sense. Toby's jaw clenched at the thought of another man bedding her, but like he'd been doing all day, he tamped down that possessive urge. He had no right to it, and if he didn't want to hurt this woman, he'd better keep any primal tendencies where she was concerned at bay.

"We can talk all you want." She smiled softly, leaning a little closer. "In the morning. Because I have a feeling tonight any talking will consist of dirty words muttered in the heat of passion while you fuck me hard."

He groaned. How the hell was he going to play with her and not fuck her? His resolve to do the noble thing was wavering, and he still needed answers. As she kissed his neck he couldn't help but agree with her. Tomorrow. He'd get the answers tomorrow.

CHAPTER SIX

Krista sat on Toby's lap, playing cards with all the guys and doing her best to stay focused. She knew she felt out of her element last night. Tonight, she felt like a completely different person.

Not that she was pretending to be something she wasn't. She knew she had a sexual side buried beneath her sheltered exterior, but she'd never embraced it before. So she had to fight her tendencies to run up to her room, change into some sweats, take out her contacts, put on her glasses, and read a book. Her little pep talk with Mikaela this afternoon had helped her muster up the courage to come in this room and walk straight over to Toby, but within minutes that confidence waned.

Biting her lip as she looked at the cards, she wondered if she was overdoing it. She wanted to be irresistible to Toby and show the other guys just who exactly she had eyes for, but at the same time, she didn't want to throw herself at Toby. What if he rejected her again?

And what if he didn't believe the story she'd conjured up about her fake boyfriend? God, why in the world Mikaela was insisting she keep up that ruse, Krista hadn't the foggiest idea. But even though Mikaela wasn't a senior partner, she did outrank Krista and Krista was here working on her cases. If she stayed on Mikaela's good side, then only good would come of that at the office. But she hated lying to Toby. What if something real developed with him? He'd be pissed when he found out she'd been lying to him. Of course, he could also be thrilled to learn she was an available woman.

But they'd never even get to that point without Krista coaxing Toby since he was obviously some knight in shining armor, allowing her to maintain her virtue. Which brought her back to her immediate worry— was she coming on too strong?

He pulled her close and nibbled on her ear. "What's wrong, baby?"

She exhaled heavily, not realizing she'd been holding her breath, his gentle concern giving her renewed hope that she was on the right course. She had to stop second-guessing herself. She obviously had something going on that appealed to this man. After turning to him, she smiled, then leaned her head against his.

"Nothing. Just a long day."

He kissed her temple. "C'mon, I'll walk you to your room." He started to get up, but Krista put her hands on his shoulders to stay him.

"No." *Crap.* She didn't want this night to end. She wasn't tired. She was horny, and the day had been long because she'd spent a good part of it fantasizing about what Toby looked like naked. "Um, I, er—"

"Toby," Mikaela interrupted, and Krista gave her a grateful look. "Why don't you take Krista for a walk? We've been cooped up here all day, and I'm sure she'd love to get some fresh air." She turned to Krista. "The stars are beautiful out here. Looks like you can reach up and touch them."

Krista smiled at Mikaela then turned to Toby. "I'd like that."

He half-smiled at her, scooting his chair to the side so they could more easily get up. "Then let's go. I've taken enough of their money for one night."

"You were just lucky," Rob grumbled.

Toby looked at her, and the intensity of his gaze made her heart beat faster, her tummy tingle. God, she was so head-over-heels for this man. It didn't make sense. She hardly knew him, but she couldn't deny it.

"No," Toby started, keeping his eyes on Krista, "I *am* lucky."

She couldn't breathe. If he wasn't careful, she'd jump his bones right here and now.

"C'mon, baby. Let me show you the grounds."

After she mumbled some goodbyes, Toby took her by the hand and led her out of the room. He complimented her on her outfit and engaged in other small talk as they walked outside, all the while rubbing soft circles on the back of her hand. She smiled up at him like some lovesick teenager facing her first crush, and in some ways that was exactly what he was. She couldn't remember feeling this way about another person before.

"Oh, wow," Krista breathed, looking up at the sky as soon as they cleared the porch. "It's so beautiful."

"Yeah, it really is. I guess I'm just used to seeing it all the time."

They took a few more steps, but Krista couldn't take her eyes off the sky. It was flooded with twinkling lights, like large diamonds in the sky. And the moon was huge, too. She could make out the craters with surprising clarity.

As they walked, Krista asked Toby about the family business, and he told her about tree farming, not leaving out any of the strenuous details. She couldn't help but smile at him when he spoke of his family and the livelihood that supported their way of life. He loved the outdoors, but she figured all of his brothers did. As they walked around the other side of the house and farther away from it, she started to get a little nervous. Not because of being alone with Toby, but because she was in the middle of a dang forest. And now they were standing at the edge of the woods.

"Is it safe out here?" she asked, her voice trembling.

He pulled her up against his chest, stroking her hair. "I won't let anything get you," he murmured.

She stared up into his eyes, their sparkle rivaling the starry sky, and leaned closer, licking her lips.

He groaned, bent down, and brushed his lips against hers. "I can't explain what it is you do to me, Krista."

He didn't give her an opportunity to respond. He took her mouth in a heated kiss, and she returned it, pouring all she had to give into it. She wound her arms around his neck and popped up on her toes to get as close to him as possible, loving the feel of his body against the full length of hers.

Hard muscle met soft curves, and it felt like a perfect match. Toby's hands slid into her hair, fisting it as he kissed her harder, and the little sting on her scalp pulsed straight to her pussy. She moaned, her hands digging into his hair.

Toby growled, grabbing her by the waist and spinning her. Her back landed against the rough bark of a tree, but she didn't care. She just didn't want him to stop.

It was clear he had no intentions of doing that.

He rubbed his hard cock against her belly, but that wasn't where she wanted it. She lifted one leg to hook over his hip, and he reached down and grabbed her knee to hold her leg up.

It still wasn't enough.

She started raising her other leg, so Toby took her cue and grabbed her ass, lifting her right where she wanted to be. She undulated against his cock as she wrapped both legs around his waist.

"Oh, fuck, baby." He thrust against her, trailing kisses along her neck, as the bark bit into her back.

"Toby," she breathed. She was at a loss for words, too overwhelmed with every sensation. She wanted him to take her right here, and the way he was grinding himself against her as he sucked and bit the sensitive skin where her neck met her shoulder only made her want it that much more.

She shoved her hand between them and pulled his shirt out from his pants. He hissed when she burrowed her hand beneath his jeans, not bothering to un-buckle his belt or unsnap his pants. She stroked his cock, and he thrust his hips, pushing himself against her arm that was between them while he snaked his hand down her low-cut top, seeking out a breast with one hand and squeezing her ass with the other. He took possession of her mouth again with a breathless, frantic kiss.

She worked his cock, jacking him off with a firm, quick motion while he played with her nipple and ate at her lips. Then his head tore away from her on a growl. "Oh, shit, shit. I'm gonna—stop, stop, baby." He seized her hand. "I don't want to come like this." He dug his head into the crook of her neck, panting.

She rested her cheek against his hair, trying to get herself together as it seemed Toby was trying to do. She wasn't sure what she should say. She definitely wasn't ready to call it a night. Oh, hell no.

He leaned back, kissing her forehead, his lips lingering there. "Come with me to my cabin?" He tried phrasing it as a ques-tion, but the look in his eyes was de-manding.

"Cabin? I thought you had a room in the main house."

He kissed her gently, a soft brush of his lips against hers. "I do. But we all have our own cabins. After Josh and Mikaela got married, they picked one out and said they needed some privacy, being very insistent on claiming one particular cabin for some reason, so Dad told us all to pick one out." He nuzzled her hair. "I want some privacy with you tonight."

"Just tonight?"

He chuckled. "No, but it's a start."

Why that answer delighted her so much, she couldn't say.

———

TOBY UNLOCKED the cabin with the key that was resting atop the doorjamb. He didn't know why he felt so nervous bringing Krista here.

Bullshit. He knew exactly why he was nervous. He hadn't been with a woman in years. He'd been two seconds away from ripping her jeans off and fucking her against that tree, but now that he'd been granted a respite, he couldn't help but wonder if he should go through with this. Not just because she was a virgin, but because deep down he knew, just knew, he wouldn't be able to let her go once they'd taken this step.

And that scared the shit out of him because he wanted her more than he'd ever wanted another woman.

"Nice."

His head snapped up to look at her. She was surveying his cabin with a look of honest appreciation.

"Yeah, well, it's the biggest one. Not that I picked it for that reason. It's the closest to the woods."

"I like being close to the woods." She walked toward him, slowly peeling off her loose flannel shirt and leaving her in that sexy tank top. His mouth dried at the sight of her. Then she whipped that shirt off, too, and he shut his eyes briefly, too overwhelmed. God, he needed this to be slow for her, but what he really wanted to do was rip off her clothes, throw her on the ground, and fuck her so hard, she'd give him her throat in a sign of total submission. Then he wanted to sink his fangs right —*fuck!* He couldn't think about that. She could not be his mate, damn it. Thank God, she was a taken woman. Maybe he'd just nix the whole conversation with her about her boyfriend and have her e-mail him the answers once she got back to her office. The idea that her answer could ignite his need to claim her was too risky to chance.

She bent over to pull off her boots, socks, and jeans, and he stepped back and leaned against the desk that was behind him, gripping it to keep from touching her. He'd let her set the pace. He had to because if he touched her right now, he'd lose all control.

She reached behind her and unclasped the pink bra, and it tumbled to the floor.

"Fuck," he breathed, squeezing his eyes shut, white-knuckling the edge of the desk. Krista had a gorgeous body, and he'd had his mouth on those beautiful nipples last night. His mouth watered as he remembered the taste of her, and he immediately wanted to taste her everywhere. At this rate he wasn't going to last five seconds once he touched her.

"Why are you all the way over there?" she asked softly, moving toward him again.

"Because if I touch you right now, I

won't be gentle." His voice was so hoarse he barely recognized it.

She stepped up against him, her bare breasts rubbing against his disheveled shirt. "Who said I want you to be gentle?"

He groaned, his head falling back as she unbuttoned his shirt. "I'm not playing, baby. It's been a long time for me, and you need an easier lover for your first time."

She hummed against his chest as she kissed the flesh she'd uncovered, spreading his shirt wide open. "What I need is for you to take your clothes off." She stepped away, backing in to the exposed alcove that worked as his bedroom. From this angle, he could see her situating herself on his bed. He stalked toward her, stopping at the corner wall and leaning against it to watch her. "Are you going to undress, or do I need to tease you a little?"

Oh, hell. He didn't need any incentive to touch her. Did she not understand he was trying to calm his raging need to take her hard? He had every intention of fucking her—any noble notion he had of her keeping her virginity was long gone—but he was trying to get his wits about him.

He must've taken too long to respond

because that little vixen lifted her butt in the air and pulled her panties down, leaving them wrapped around her thighs. With her knees bent and legs spread as far as the barrier of her panties allowed, Krista trailed her hand down her belly and slipped her finger into the wet folds of her pussy.

The sight of her touching herself was the last straw. Toby barely registered ripping off his shirt and divesting himself of the rest of this clothing, but what felt like instantaneously he was naked and perched on the bed beside her, kissing her knee and caressing her other thigh.

Then he grabbed her panties and tore them from her body.

Krista gasped and started closing her legs, but Toby pried them apart and fell between them, his mouth hovering over her core.

"T-Toby?"

He didn't answer, not verbally anyway. Instead he lowered his head and licked her from her asshole to her clit. Taste. He wanted to taste her everywhere. He did it again and again, and with each pass, he increased his pace. He'd never tasted anything as sweet as her, and he needed more. He began fucking her with his tongue, her tangy honey spilling onto it as he stabbed into her pussy. She writhed beneath him, her moans piercing his soul and electrifying his body. His balls ached and his cock painfully engorged, but he couldn't stop tasting her to seek his own relief. Not yet. He needed to imprint her very essence into himself.

He tore his mouth away from her pussy and licked her thighs, kissed her knees, bit her calves, and sucked her toes, working his way from one leg to the other. When he reached her core again, he bypassed it to nip her tummy, then delve his tongue into her belly button, suck her nipples, lick her neck, and nibble on her ears. Everywhere. He had to taste her everywhere. He shoved his tongue into her mouth, kissing her greedily, and she moaned, throwing her arms around his neck. But he wasn't done exploring her body with his mouth.

Not even close.

He pulled away and flipped her over, treating her backside to the same attention her front had received, leaving no inch untouched. And she seemed to have relished his ministrations, for her moans turned to cries when he bit her ass, so he did it again. Harder.

Mark. I have to mark her.

He covered her with his body, grabbing her hair and fisting it to the side. He bit her neck, wishing it were his fangs piercing her skin and not his teeth. He understood she was taken, so he wouldn't cross that line. But his animal and his humanity seemed to agree that having her as a mate would be the ultimate gift. If only he could take her. But he couldn't. So, he'd mark her everywhere, show everyone who she belonged to, if only for a short while.

He turned her again, too impatient to prolong their joining. He grabbed a condom out of his nightstand and rolled it on, thankful Josh had insisted on stocking up on them. When Toby settled between her legs, he took her mouth in a possessive kiss as he positioned his cock at her opening. He wasn't sure how he was able to go slow at this point, but he did, nudging into her gently.

As if his body knew what hers needed without conscious thought. Just like it would do if she were his mate, if she were meant to be his always.

He shook his head, trying to dislodge that thought. He couldn't think about that. She wasn't available for him to take. Not in that way. But he'd take what he could. He'd have her now.

She gasped as he breached her, rolling her hips to meet his thrusts.

"Am I hurting you, baby?" he kissed her temple.

She shook her head and grabbed his ass, pulling him toward her. "More."

He groaned and pushed all the way into her with one long thrust, giving her what she wanted, what he needed. She groaned, her nails digging into his flesh as he began to fuck her. Slowly at first, then with more urgency. Her pussy was like a velvet vise, fisting around his cock. He'd never felt anything more perfect. It was heaven.

But it was also hell. He didn't know how he'd be able to give her up once she was gone. With his head buried into her neck, he growled his need to claim her, his finesse waning.

"Oh, God, Toby, Toby, Toby," she

chanted, his name on her lips a caress of his soul. He could feel her pussy spasm around his dick, and he damn-near came from the combination of all the sensations.

"Oh, God, Oh, God, I'm coming." She screamed and sank her little teeth into his shoulder, and his head fell back on a roar as his fangs descended. He plowed into her as he exploded with the strongest climax he'd ever experienced before.

His thrusts stopped, and he looked down at her. She had her beautiful eyes closed, a vision of true beauty. He wanted to ask how she was feeling, but he couldn't as long as he was sporting fangs. This had been the first time his animal had ever roared to the forefront like that. He'd have to ask Josh if it'd ever happened to him. He could ask his other brothers, but Toby didn't want the knowing, angered looks. Josh could be honest with him without viewing him as competition.

As he continued to stare at Krista, he was taking a risk just looking at her. She could look up and notice the bumps where his lips covered the evidence of his animal side. But he had to look at her.

With one last gaze of her face and

flushed chest, Toby ducked his head into the crook of her neck. He wanted to bite her, but he wouldn't. He took in deep breaths and willed his fangs to retract, the effort being much harder than he'd anticipated.

Once it was safe, he kissed her shoulder, and finally asked what he'd been wanting to. "How are you feeling, baby? Was I too rough?"

She stroked his back lazily. "No. I feel wonderful. You feel wonderful."

He shifted above her, looking into her eyes now that they were open. "You're so beautiful. Perfect."

She blushed, giving him a timid smile.

He couldn't have her being shy after everything they'd just gone through. He leaned down, kissing her nose. "Sexy." He kissed her cheek. "Irresistible." He nibbled on her ear, and she giggled. He smiled against her in return. *Mine.* He wanted to say it, but he didn't. It was too dangerous to think like that. He needed to figure out how to get ahold of his emotions.

He eased off her to take care of the condom. He needed to talk to Josh tonight before things got too carried away with Krista.

He should be out running with his brother, so as soon as Krista fell asleep, Toby would seek out his brother's help.

Because he feared things had already gone too far with her and he didn't want to stop.

CHAPTER SEVEN

Toby eased the back patio door shut, pulled off his robe, and shifted. God, he loved being in his mountain lion form. He felt free, and all the stresses of everyday life disappeared. All that mattered was food, sleep, and mate. With that thought, he turned to look through the glass door of his cabin. He couldn't see Krista, but he knew she was in there. He wanted to go to her, so he turned and ran into the woods. The sooner he talked to his brother, the sooner he could be back in bed with the woman who was stealing his heart.

It was too soon. She'd only just arrived. How could he have these kinds of feelings brewing for her already? As he ran, he found a squirrel and chased it up a tree.

The little shit was faster, so he climbed down and kept running.

He heard leaves rustling on the ground around the bend, so he headed that way, figuring it'd be one of his brothers. When he ran around the corner, he came upon two mountain lions tussling. At first he figured it was a couple of his brothers, but then one of them tried to mount the other.

Oh, shit. He'd walked in on Josh and Mikaela about to mate in their feral forms. Not good.

Josh spun around, hissing at Toby. *Mine!*

Sorry. I-I wanted to talk to you, but I see you're busy right now. He started to back up. Realistically, Josh knew that none of his brothers would try to take Mikaela away from him, but Toby understood that, in beast form, logic was a little harder to grasp.

Josh made a frustrated feline growl, shaking his head to the side as if it hurt. *I'll meet you at your cabin in a few minutes.*

Toby wanted to argue that he'd rather not talk there, but he was smart enough not to argue with his brother right now. Coming between a lion and his lioness could just cause one big catfight. He'd just hang around outside the cabin, waiting for Josh, so as not to disturb Krista. *Okay.*

He turned and trotted back to his cabin. The feline cries rent the air around him as Josh claimed his wife in that primal way. The fact that those two were mating in their feline forms meant only one thing. They were trying to get pregnant. Toby's dad had always told them mating in that form was reserved for procreation just like in the wild. People were the only animals that fucked for fun—no other animals did. There was no proof that they couldn't get a female pregnant in human form, but mating in animal form only served that one purpose.

When he got back to his cabin, Toby shifted and put on his robe. He sat on the railing, looking up at the stars. Time passed —he didn't know how much. But eventually, Josh came strolling up to the back porch.

"Sorry, man. I didn't mean to interrupt."

Josh shrugged. "Just keep what you saw to yourself, okay? We want a baby, but we don't want to tell everyone just yet. We'd rather wait until Mikaela gets pregnant before announcing anything."

"Oh, hey. I understand. Totally. My lips are sealed."

Josh's shoulders relaxed like he was relieved to hear Toby wouldn't spread their secret. "So, what's bothering you?" Josh asked as he climbed the stairs and leaned against the railing next to Toby.

"It's this thing with Krista. I like her, man. A lot. I know she's not available, which is a good thing," he added quickly. "But, er, I'm having a hard time accepting I can't have her. I'm not sure how I'll be able to let her go when she has to leave."

Josh sighed. "Look, maybe you feel this way because of the whole virgin thing—"

"What the hell?" Toby barked, turning on his brother. How the fuck did he know about that?

Josh raised his hands in a placating gesture. "Sorry, bro. Girls talk. And so do spouses. I mean... *I* don't talk. Could just be a wife thing. I don't know. I just sit and listen." He chuckled.

Toby nodded on an exhale, understanding.

"Anyway,   Mikaela   said   Krista's

boyfriend is in the military. Some special ops dude. He's gone all the time, but they grew up together. They plan on marrying each other, but he doesn't want her tied to him with the danger of his job. This is his last service. He's not upping again, and once he gets out, they'll be exclusive."

"When does he get out?" Toby heard himself asking but was too numb to feel the words coming out.

"Eighteen months. They're planning to get married about six months after he returns."

He made a noncommittal noise, looking away. He knew she was involved, but the evidence of it stung. After learning she'd been a virgin, he'd hoped—*No!* Didn't matter what he'd hoped.

"You ever fuck a woman and your fangs pop out?"

Josh chuckled. "Oh, yeah. Those damn things were a pain in the ass when I was sleeping with Mikaela before we mated. I even bit myself once to keep from biting her."

Toby whirled. "What about with other women? Someone not your mate?"

Josh frowned. "No, I never wanted anybody but—son of a bitch! Are you telling me that happened to you with Krista?"

Toby nodded.

"Shit, man. That's major."

"That's what I was worried about. I tried to stay away from her. You know I did. But it's like I'm drawn to her, and I have no power to fight that attraction."

"You have to. She'll be leaving here when Mikaela is finished needing her with her lawyer stuff. She has a life away from here. A *love* away from here."

Toby's chest ached. He didn't want to think about all that. Not now. "What do I do?"

Josh gripped Toby's shoulder. "You enjoy her while you can. Don't worry about the future. These things have a way of working themselves out, but if it doesn't work out in your favor, then worry about that after she's gone."

That was exactly what he'd do. What choice did he have?

———

KRISTA AWOKE to the smell of scrumptious bacon, and her stomach growled like she hadn't eaten in days. She eased out of the bed and felt the delicious soreness at the apex of her thighs. She smiled as her hand drifted to the source. She wasn't a virgin anymore. It was a surreal feeling, but that thought took a backseat to the one of Toby. Of him smiling at her, talking to her, and loving her. Loving? *Making* love was what she meant to think.

She looked around the floor for her shirt, but saw his draped over the dresser. She grabbed it and put it on, only buttoning a few of the middle buttons. She rolled up the sleeves as she walked into the main room which housed the living room and kitchen. Toby had his back to her, standing at the stove. She walked over to him and slid her arms around his chest, hugging him from behind. "Good morning," she mumbled against his back.

He clutched her hands and brought them up to his face, kissing them. "Good morning, baby." Then he turned and kissed her sweetly.

She pulled away and covered her mouth. "I haven't brushed my teeth," she mumbled through her hand.

He chuckled as he pointed to the door.

"I had Jeffery bring your things over here. You can brush your teeth and take out your contacts. I know your eyes must be sore leaving them in all night." He leaned down and kissed each eyelid before turning back to the bacon.

She gaped at his back. "You-You had my things brought over here?"

He immediately turned back around, looking contrite. "I'm sorry. I want to be with you as long as I can." Something dark flashed across his eyes, and his jaw clenched. Then he took a deep breath and smiled apologetically at her. "I should've asked you first, but I wanted you to have everything you need when you woke up."

She wasn't concerned about staying here. In fact, she loved the idea! She was just shocked he'd want her to stay with him while she was here. Granted, she didn't have much experience with men, but what she'd read in all those online magazines was that men didn't like clingy women. Maybe Toby was different. "Okay. I'd like that very much."

"Good. Then it's settled. And the bacon's done. All I have to do now is cook the eggs."

He winked and smiled, and those sexy-assed dimples popped out. God, he was the hottest man she'd ever seen. Unable to stop herself, she rose up on her toes and licked one divot.

His breath caught, and then he chuckled. "What are you doing?"

"Licking your dimple."

"Mmm. I like it." He turned his head, giving her his other cheek. She licked that one, too.

"Tell me, Mr. Woods, do you have any other dimples I can lick?"

He sucked in a breath and turned his head to look at her. She smiled coyly at him, contemplating where she wanted to put her mouth next. Since he'd taken the pan off the burner, she could play with him a little without having to worry about burning down his house. He'd spent what felt like an eternity tasting her last night, and she was curious what he tasted like. She'd obviously never given a guy a blowjob, but as she thought about taking Toby's cock into her mouth, she felt a restlessness to drop to her knees and give him the best head he'd ever had. There was no reason not to. She was a little too sore for sex anyway, so this would be the perfect time to try it out.

So she eased to her knees, and he gasped when she tugged his sleep pants down. His dick was partially erect, but getting harder by the second. "Baby, you don't —" He stopped on a hiss when she licked the head of his cock.

"I want to taste you, Toby." She wrapped her hand around his cock and looked up at him from her kneeling position at his feet. "Please," she breathed as she gave his cock a gentle stroke.

He groaned and nodded as he sifted his hands through her hair.

A twinge of insecurity prickled her. Toby was an experienced man, and she didn't know what she was doing. Maybe she should've practiced this on her vibrator.

"I-I, um... Let me know if I do something wrong, okay? I want this to be good for you."

He caressed her cheek, and the emotion in his eyes startled her. If she didn't know any better, she'd think he was falling in love with her.

"If your hot little mouth is anywhere near my dick, it'll be good, baby," he whispered. "But I'll help guide you if it'll make you feel better."

She nodded, relieved that he understood and didn't say anything to further her embarrassment. She shifted, bringing her mouth to his cock and licking it again. She closed her mouth around the head and sucked gently. He groaned, clutching her hair.

"That's it. Fuck, Krista, your mouth feels so good."

His praise eased her concerns some more, so she opened her mouth and took more of him in. She moved back and forth, taking as much of his erection as she could into her mouth, lapping at him with her tongue and sucking him at the tip.

He hissed and rocked his hips. "Oh, yes. Move your hand, baby. Stroke my cock while you suck it." He groaned and tightened his hands in her hair when she'd complied.

He had an earthy taste that fed her senses. She felt her sensitive pussy getting wet and her clit swelling with need. She sucked him harder and faster as if that'd alleviate the growing ache between her legs.

His hips were pumping in time with her thrusts as if he were fucking her mouth, which in essence he was. Thinking of it in that sense felt so erotic that she groaned around the mouthful of cock she was eagerly sucking.

"Fuck! That felt good. Squeeze my balls with your other hand, baby."

Frantic to please him, she reached up and squeezed his sac, rolling his balls with one hand while she jerked him off with the other. His cock grew even harder as he held her head still. Then he fucked her mouth in earnest, groaning and panting with effort.

She was so damn turned-on that she let go of his balls and shoved her hand under the shirt she had on. She found her clit and rubbed it fast as she could.

"Oh, fuck yeah, fuck yeah, baby. Make yourself come for me."

Her pussy throbbed as her orgasm claimed her. She moaned around his cock, and he threw his head back and roared. The first spurt of his release startled her, but she worked her throat as she swallowed all he had to give.

He slumped back and grabbed the counter, sated. "Shit!" He jumped away, startling her as his cock jerked out of her mouth. He shook his hand. "Damn, that was hot."

She smiled at him. "You should watch where you put your hands. There's a hot stove behind you." She started to stand, and he reached down to help her.

"You should watch where you put your hands. There's a hot cock in front of you." He laughed, nuzzling her hair.

She giggled. "That was cheesy."

"I'm full of cheese, baby. Get used to it. For as long as you're here, we'll be joined at the hip. Cheese and all."

She smiled against his chest. She could get used to being around him.

Cheese and all.

CHAPTER EIGHT

KRISTA WAS in love with Toby. She wasn't sure when it happened, but she was sure it had. Over the last month, they'd been as inseparable as he'd warned after their first night together. Oh, they still went their separate ways during the workday. After all, she was here to help Mikaela with her caseload while she orchestrated the purchase of the adjacent Caldwell Tree Farm. Luckily, the hiccup with the purchase only delayed the sale a couple of weeks and was now scheduled to close a week from Friday. But Krista couldn't help but appreciate the interruption because she would've left two days ago if it hadn't happened.

Every morning, Toby had insisted on

cooking her breakfast. When she worried what his father would think of her missing breakfast at the main house, Toby brushed off her concerns with sweet kisses, telling her that Mikaela hadn't always come down to breakfast when she first arrived. Plus, he'd argued that if he cooked, then they wouldn't have to get up as early. So, he had cooked her breakfast, burning a few here and there, and she'd gladly eaten everything because he genuinely wanted to do it for her.

If their mornings had been filled with lazy kisses and laughable breakfast experiments, their nights had been nothing but the hot monkey sex she'd hoped to one day experience. Only better.

Way better.

Toby was an attentive, patient lover. He'd introduced her to just about every position imaginable, taking her with care regardless of how intense some of their couplings had been, fucking her well into the night. Every night.

On a few occasions she'd woken up expecting to find him snuggled up against her, blanketing her body like usual, but she'd been all alone. She'd searched the cabin only to come up without any trace of where he'd been. The first time it'd happened, she figured he would've said something about it the following morning, but he hadn't. She thought about asking where he went in the middle of the night but decided it was probably none of her business. It wasn't as if he were going off on some assignation. The only woman around here besides her was Mikaela. So, she let it go. She had bigger concerns than wondering where Toby slipped away to during the middle of the night.

Like this whole boyfriend lie she was living. Maybe she hadn't pressed Toby about his secret because she felt guilty about her own.

As she walked into the office she shared with Mikaela on this Monday morning, she couldn't stop thinking about how silly the whole thing seemed. When Mikaela had told her about Josh's brothers' fear of commitment and hinted at the possibility Krista could enjoy some casual sex, she'd been excited about the idea. Okay, so she'd been scared witless, but deep down she'd been harboring nervous energy that could've easily been construed as excitement. And she was at least willing to consider the possibility. She never imagined she'd meet the man of her dreams and fall in love within a month. Now after spending this time with Toby, she felt like a fraud.

"Good morning, Krista," Mikaela said as Krista strolled into the office. "Or should I say good afternoon?" She chuckled.

"Ha-ha. It's nine not noon. Big difference." She slumped into her chair, staring at the few case files left that needed any attention, and really, the work wasn't pressing.

"What's with the long face?" Mikaela asked softly. Krista looked at her, realizing they were really friends now. Over the past few weeks Toby hadn't been the only person Krista had gotten close to. Her long workdays were filled with female camaraderie she'd sorely been lacking before coming out here. Although she knew she could turn to Mikaela before, now she embraced that trust built between them.

She sighed, glancing at her coffee cup and willing it to be filled with the delicious ebony liquid so she wouldn't have to actually get up. Her expression must've been more forlorn than she realized because

Mikaela got up and grabbed Krista's cup with an exaggerated roll of her eyes. "Good gravy, girl. Here. I'll get you some. Just start spilling your guts. I can listen and pour at the same time."

"I want to tell Toby the truth. About me not having a boyfriend, I mean." When Mikaela whirled to pin Krista with a stare, she continued. "I understand what you told me before coming out here, but I don't think Toby will dump me because I don't have a boyfriend. I think we've moved passed the casual sex phase... like almost right away."

Mikaela turned back to the coffee pot, filled Krista's cup, and brought it over to her before sitting on the corner of her desk. "No," she said softly, "he won't break up with you because you don't have a boyfriend. But do you want to risk that happening, because it might if you tell him the truth now?"

Krista took a deep breath. "I've thought about that, too, and, well, I know this mess is of my own making." She narrowed her eyes at Mikaela. "Instigated by you, of course, but I can't fix it if I don't come clean."

Mikaela nodded. "Okay, how about this —you keep quiet until after you leave. Stay in touch with Toby, and when the time's right, tell him you're not getting married and you want to be with him."

"That's still lying."

"Jesus, Krista. You're an attorney. Think like one. What I suggested isn't a lie because (A.) you're not getting married and (B.) you do want Toby."

"That's lying by omission."

"Semantics."

Krista groaned with frustration as she leaned back into her chair and picked up her coffee. She sipped it lightly.

"How did you know you wanted Josh?"

Mikaela smiled with a faraway look on her face. "I just did. I'd recently broken off an engagement, as you know, when I was assigned to revamp Thomas's will. Of course I was drawn to Josh right away, but I had my secret. I wanted him, but I was here on an assignment. He wanted me too. Boy, did he want me!" She laughed. "He came onto me that first night then dodged me. I didn't know what to make of it at the time, but everything makes sense to me now." She turned and gave Krista a pointed look.

"Everything will fall into place with you, too. If you let it. Just keep quiet for now. You leave next week. Why chance pissing him off when you can enjoy the remaining time you have here?"

She had a point, damn it. Krista didn't want to ruin the relationship she had with Toby. Even if they were just playing house for now, it'd been the best time of her life. "I love him," she murmured. Her eyes shot to Mikaela, panicking that she'd said it out loud.

Mikaela smiled at her. "Then love him and keep him as long as you can. And talk to him after you've had some time away from here to make sure it's truly how you feel."

Good advice, but Krista was already certain. No time apart would ever change how she felt about Toby. But a week from Friday she'd be gone. Did she want to chance disrupting the only peace and love she'd ever felt in her life when she could live it just a little bit longer? No. She knew that made her incredibly selfish, but she'd need these memories to get her through the rest of her life.

"Okay," she breathed. "I'll wait."

Mikaela nodded. "Good. Now we don't really have a lot going on today. I'm not expecting a call from the title company until tomorrow. Why don't you and I go see the guys in action? It really is amazing watching them plant and cut the trees."

"Sure, sounds great." Only she couldn't muster real enthusiasm. It should've been easy for her to fake it since she was a big ol' fraud anyway.

———

TOBY WIPED the sweat from his brow as he tried dislodging debris from the wheels of the tractor, grunting and straining with effort.

"Hold up there, hawse." Toby turned to see Josh walking toward him with some tree pruners.

"You rock, man," Toby said as he stood and caught his breath.

"Can't argue there." Josh chuckled, and he bent down and started to chop the mangled limbs. While he worked, he glanced up at Toby. "You wanna come over to my cabin one night this weekend? I was thinking we could cook out, do the double-date thing before Krista has to go back."

A crushing weight landed on Toby's chest at the reminder of Krista's schedule. He'd been avoiding the reality of her departure, knowing it was stupid not to face that fact head-on, but damn it, he just couldn't bring himself to accept there'd come a day when he'd wake up and she would not be there. She'd rocked his world, not wiggling her way into his life. Oh, no, she'd forced her way in with what seemed like no effort at all. And with her, he'd found himself surrounded by pleasure like none other. Her presence in his life a balm to his lonely soul. She was the other part of him.

He loved her.

God, he was so screwed. A few times he'd almost told her how he felt, but at the last second, he'd found the strength to resist confessing his heart and soul to her. She belonged to another man, and his mountain lion was in agony with the knowledge that he'd never get to claim his mate. Because Krista was the only mate for him.

And once she was gone, he'd go back to how life was before. But he'd never be the same. His mountain lion wasn't the only part of him hurting.

"Toby?"

He blinked looking at Josh. *Oh, shit,* he'd asked about dinner. "Yeah, sure. I'll ask her, but I'm sure she won't mind. How about Saturday?" He tried being nonchalant but had no idea if he was.

"Works for me."

"What're you two dickheads doing? Quit pussyfooting around with that and come on," Rob said as he came around the tractor.

Josh stood. "Almost got it. Just having a little trouble with this branch."

Rob leaned down. "Let me." He reached for the branch just as the tree pruner slipped. It sliced across his arm, and he yelled, grabbing his wound.

"Fuck! Are you okay?" Josh asked, turning toward him. Toby stepped up so he could see how badly his brother was hurt.

But as soon as he did, his adrenaline kicked in double time. Not only had Rob's fangs descended, but his pupils had turned into cat-eye slits. "Rob, you have to calm down," Toby said as he grabbed his shoulder. "We'll get you inside and cleaned up."

Rob roared and lunged for Toby, shifting before he reached him. He landed with his paws on Toby's chest. Toby didn't want to hurt his brother because he knew it was an animalistic reaction to the injury he'd just received. So, he grabbed him by the scruff, trying to pull him off.

As soon as he grabbed him, Toby heard a scream. A very feminine scream. As he turned, he saw Mikaela and Krista stopped on the dirt road staring right at them. *Shit.* This was so not good.

Then Rob hissed in their direction and tried pushing off Toby's chest, eyes on the ladies. "No!" Toby yelled. *Rob, chill out. Don't you fucking dare try to attack—*

Toby's protest died as Rob got loose and charged the girls. *What the fuck?* They weren't a threat to him, and he knew that.

He had to protect Krista. She was his! There was a roar beside him as Josh shifted and chased after Rob.

Stay away from my mate!

Toby started running after Josh. Then Mikaela shifted right next to Krista and ran toward Rob. *Fuck, fuck, fuck!*

Back off, Mikaela. It's not you I want, Rob growled as he neared the women.

Toby knew what he had to do. He couldn't fight it, not when his love was in danger. He shifted, his clothes ripping off his body just like the others, and ran as fast as he could. He couldn't look at Krista. He didn't want to see the terror, the confusion in her eyes. A closely guarded family secret—and Rob had just fucked that up. He should've known after the first several days of being with Krista when Rob and Jack had finally backed off that it wouldn't last. They'd never had a female on the property this long—taken or otherwise—unless she was one of their mates. But Krista was still unavailable, so Rob couldn't claim her. His behavior was uncharacteristic of their kind. Unless the injury ignited some fight-or-flight-or-fuck reaction.

Toby reached Rob just as he jumped over Mikaela and tackled Krista, knocking her to the ground. Toby roared, barreling into his brother's side and toppling him over beside Krista. He rolled them over several feet while Mikaela and Josh shielded her from further attacks.

Bro, what the fuck? She's taken. Taken!

I know, Toby. I'm not going to claim her, but I want to play with her.

Oh, fuck you! You ain't going anywhere near her; you hear me? She's mine!

"Rob!" Jack bellowed. "Stand down. You don't want to do this. You're stronger than your lion."

Toby wasn't sure when Jack had arrived, but when Rob's struggles lessened, he was glad Jack had been able to reason with him.

Rob finally stopped struggling altogether, going limp underneath Toby. *Sorry. Shit. I-I don't know what got into me. And, fuck, my arm hurts.*

You're getting blood all over me, Toby said as he licked his brother's wound to help the blood coagulate.

Rob hissed at him, but Toby knew it was because of the pain. *We need to get you out of here.*

"I called Dad. The doctor's on his way," Jack said, obviously hearing the mental communication.

Toby moved off Rob and looked at Krista. Jack was standing next to her, grasping her upper arms as if holding her in place. Toby growled low in his throat at the sight of another man touching his woman.

"None of that," Jack warned.

Damn it, he knew his brother was right, but he still didn't like it. But when he finally looked at Krista, saw her pale face, wide eyes, he suppressed his urge to continue protecting her. Jack wasn't a threat, and the last thing Toby wanted to do was scare her even more than she already was.

Fuck, I've got a lot of explaining to do.

I'll do it, Mikaela said. *Just, er, let me run home and shift first. I don't want to walk back in the buff.*

I need to be the one to tell her. He wanted to be the one to tell her.

I understand, Toby, but I think it'd be better if you let me ease her into your conversation.

She's right, Josh agreed. *Let her smooth things over, then you can talk to Krista.*

Toby didn't like the idea of losing sight of her. What if she ran off without talking to him first? But as he thought about it, he knew Mikaela had a point. They were friends, and his sister-in-law could help Krista see things from an outside perspective since she'd once been an outsider herself. *Fine. But I'm going to follow her to your place. Jack, can you walk Krista to Josh's cabin?*

"Sure." Krista looked up at Jack, clearly seeing them communicating. "Come on, sweetheart. Mikaela wants to talk to you."

"I-I... "

"I know. This is a big surprise. But I promise all your questions will be answered."

CHAPTER NINE

Krista sat on the couch inside the cabin Mikaela shared with Josh, waiting for her friend to come and explain to her how in the hell everyone turned in to animals. She wasn't sure what they'd turned into. Some kind of cat, it'd looked like, but they sure as hell didn't look like Mr. Fuzzy Tail, her childhood kitty cat.

She was freaking out. That had to be it. Maybe she was having a nervous breakdown? If that was the case, she needed a straightjacket STAT. People didn't just up and turn into other things. That kind of shit didn't happen. And what was all that looking around at each other and Jack responding like he'd been talking to them? Either she'd lost her mind or she'd ended up in some alternate reality. Maybe her ass was still asleep and this was one fucked-up dream.

She started when Mikaela walked into the room. *Nope, no dream.* Krista was dreadfully awake. Oh, God, she was going to the funny farm.

"Don't look at me all scared like, girl. I'm still the same person I was yesterday. I just have a natural fur coat that I didn't have to skin another animal for or pay *beaucoup* bucks to get."

Krista laughed nervously. *Oh, Jesus, it was real.* They really turned into animals. She couldn't wrap her head around that knowledge, though. Mikaela looked exactly the same, yet she wasn't. She just wasn't.

Mikaela sighed, walking slowly toward Krista as if trying to corner a skittish cat. *Cat.* She giggled manically. Would she ever think of cats again and not freak the hell out?

"Ooookay, laughing's better than crying," Mikaela said, easing down onto the couch.

Krista laughed for several more seconds before trying to catch her breath. She wiped her eyes. "If I don't laugh, I think I'll scream."

"Fair enough. I promised Toby I'd let him explain everything to you. I just wanted to talk to you first. Make sure you're okay. I know this is quite a shocker."

"No shit."

"Um," Mikaela played with her hands as she looked down, and Krista frowned, never once remembering seeing Mikaela so nervous. "Look, I'm going to leave all the shifting-into-cougar stuff to Toby—"

"Cougars? I thought they had black fur."

Mikaela smiled. "Only some do, if they live deep enough in the rainforest. Toby and his brothers are mountain lion shifters." She took a deep breath then squared her shoulders. "Anyway, what I will tell you is I wasn't one until I mated with Josh. You see, they have this strong mating instinct that drives them to mate with any available female. The thing is that instinct is so uncontrolled that they could force a mating. When that happens, the newly turned female attacks back. Then there's this fight-to-the-death thing. Clearly messy." She waved her hand. "I—"

"Oh. My. God. That's why you wanted me to lie. If I came out here and they knew I didn't have a boyfriend—"

"Shhh!" Mikaela swatted her leg. "Not so loud."

"Fine," Krista gritted through a whisper. "If they knew the *truth*, then you're telling me Toby would've attacked me, turned me into a mountain lion, and then I would've fought him, and we would've killed each other? That's insane!"

"No, honey." Mikaela's eyes were sad. "What I'm telling you is if they knew the truth, every single one of them would've tried to rape you, would've forced you into a life you didn't want, and you would've been so outraged, you would've attacked as soon as you were strong enough to fight back."

Krista blanched. "What the hell?" But there was no power in her words. "W-Why did you ask me to come out here to help you if you knew the dangers?"

Mikaela shrugged. "I like you. I love them. You seemed so lonely, and I just wanted to try to put a little spice in your life while seeing if it was possible for Josh's brothers to find a mate and live through it like he did."

"So you, what? Tried to set me up with your feline family? You had no right. No. Right. To control my life like that."

Mikaela nodded. "I understand you're angry, but it's not like I tried to arrange a marriage for you. If you didn't hit it off with one of the guys, then no harm done. If you did and I was able to bring two people together who wouldn't ordinarily meet, then it was a risk I was willing to take."

"My death was a risk you were willing to take?" Krista asked incredulously.

"Oh, please. Don't be so dramatic. If you kept up with the story, then no harm done. And now you know how important it is to keep the secret. If you want to come clean with Toby, do it after you leave."

Krista sighed. What the hell was she going to do about Toby? She couldn't think about him specifically right now. It was easier to generalize this situation.

"So, they can never leave? I mean if they attack unattached women, then they're basically stuck here."

"Yeah. They're stuck, which is why I wanted to help."

Okay, Krista could see that, but she refused to acknowledge it based on principle. She was still mad at Mikaela for being deceitful, especially since they'd become friends over the last month. She'd never been this close to another woman, not ever her sister—

"Ariel."

"Huh?"

"My sister. She's a scientist. I wonder if she could formulate something that'd subdue the part of the brain that controlled rage or passion or whatever it is that triggers the need to attack available women. If the guys had access to something like that, they wouldn't be prisoners of this land."

Mikaela's eyes sparkled. "That's a great idea. Only. Um, can she be trusted with this kind of information? This is a major family secret. If the wrong people got wind of this—"

"She's a professional, Mikaela. If it'd make you feel better, we could draw up a contract outlining the penalties for divulging this kind of information."

"I knew you were a smart cookie." She smiled but then flinched. "What about her relationship status? It'd be easier if she were actually involved with someone. One less thing to worry about, you know?"

Krista shook her head. "No need to worry about that. She married Will, her high-school sweetheart. They're the kind of couple that is so lovey-dovey you wanna gag."

"Good. Call her, see when she can meet. I'd like to get started on this as soon as possible."

"Okay." Krista pulled out her cell phone and started dialing her sister's number. Focusing on a project was just the diversion she needed right now.

"You're taking this much better than I thought you would."

"Oh, I'm still pissed at you for not living by the girlfriend code and providing full disclosure, but if I think about this clinically, I don't have to accept it. Not yet."

Not until she talked to Toby. And she wasn't sure she was ready for that. Talking to him would make everything more real. Denial was much more to her liking.

Her sister didn't answer, so Krista left a message, stating she needed her help professionally.

After Krista got off the phone, she

stood. She might not be ready to confront Toby, but she had a feeling she didn't have a choice.

She was in love with him, but she didn't really know him at all. What did that say about her feelings?

She was scared to find out.

CHAPTER TEN

TOBY PACED in front of the couch at his cabin—the place where he'd shared his life with Krista for the past month. God, he didn't want to lose her now. He still had almost two weeks with her, and he needed every second of every day of her time remaining here to get his fill of her, knowing deep down he never would, but he was unable to help himself. He loved her. He wanted her. He knew it was wrong, but that didn't matter. Her happiness was now his. Her pain his. And the look on her face when she saw the scene unfold, realized what was happening, it was like a thousand daggers piercing his heart. He never wanted her to be afraid, to be hurt in any way, but in that moment he'd destroyed her confidence, her trust.

Maybe it was for the best. It wasn't like he could have her. Maybe she needed to see him for what he truly was. From the look in her eyes, she wouldn't accept easily. If he loved her as much as he believed he did, he would push her away, make her hate him so it'd be easier on her to move on with her life. But he wasn't that strong.

God, he didn't know what to do, and grinding a path into the hardwood as he paced didn't seem to be helping one bit.

He heard the front door open and spun around. "Krista," he breathed. She looked so lost, and he was frozen in place, battling the urge to run to her, unable to decide if she needed immediate comfort or space. She stared at him wearily, and he fucking hated it. "Baby—"

"Stop." Her hand flew up to cut him off. "Just explain to me what the hell is going on. All Mikaela said was that you're stuck here because of some lethal instinct to mate with available women and figured I would be safe with a boyfriend. But she didn't explain anything else."

"I." The catch in his throat made him

stop and clear it. "I think you should sit down. This might take a while."

She pursed her lips as she stared at him. After several seconds, she nodded and walked toward him; she sat on the opposite side of the couch from where he was standing. He sighed before sitting down, keeping the distance she'd put between them.

"We're mountain lion shifters through my father's side of the family," he said slowly, starting the dreadful conversation. "Or at least we assume it's a family trait since his parents died before he could ever learn the truth."

"And poof he just changed one day out of the blue?"

"Er, you'd have to ask him. We've tried, but he's quiet about his past. Only saying he was lucky our mother would have him, and that was that." He shrugged.

She nodded, looking away before making eye contact again. He didn't interrupt. Instead, he preferred to let her set the pace. "So, you've always been here. Never leaving this land?"

"Um, no. My brothers and I used to go to a public school. We were okay around females until we hit puberty. One-by-one, my parents took us out of school, not wanting to pull us all out at the same time. They wanted us to live a normal life as long as possible, so as soon as one of us started changing, they yanked that person out. Eric —he was the youngest—had the hardest time letting go. He stayed in touch with all his friends, which made it difficult to explain why he couldn't be around them ever again, but somehow Eric worked around that."

The few seconds of silence stretched into minutes as he watched and waited for her to say something again. It was agonizing, but he forced himself not to grovel at her feet, begging her to stay, or to put up emotional walls and ask her to leave. He didn't want her to hate him, and he feared there was no way around that.

"I don't even know what to say, Toby. This is so unbelievable. I mean, I know it's true. I saw it with my own eyes, but I'm having a really hard time wrapping my head around it."

He blew out a slow breath as he looked straight ahead. It was easier if he didn't look at her. "I know this is hard for you." What else could he say? *Please don't go?*

Please accept me for who I am? Please don't accept me and run away now? Nothing felt right.

"So, what made you decide to try sleeping with attached women?"

"We used to have a tutor who was married. A little old thing, but married. And Eric got to thinking maybe we could have female companionship if the lady in question was unavailable. I mean, we didn't try attacking our mother or our tutor. So he tried it, and it worked. Soon we'd developed online relationships with swingers. Dad built these cabins, so we'd have a place to fuck without being on top of each other. For a while it worked. Until one of the regulars Eric fucked came out here and told him she'd gotten divorced. He turned her, and they killed each other. We stopped bringing women around after that." He dropped his head into his hands and rubbed his face. He felt so cheap telling the woman he loved he used to bring women out here just to fuck without any emotional attachment.

"I-I think I get it."

His head snapped up. How the hell could she get it when he didn't even get it?

Whatever the hell *it* was. "Care to explain that to me?" he snapped.

She frowned at him. "I just understand your dilemma."

"My *dilemma?* Jesus, Krista, being a shifter is more than a dilemma. It's my life!"

"Okay, maybe that was the wrong word," she said quickly, throwing her hands up in placation. He could see her eyes working, as if she were thinking hard about something. "But it's not like you'd ever hurt me."

"Did you not just hear what I said about Eric? It can happen." Why did she not understand the dangers involved here?

She narrowed her eyes and put one hand on her hip. "I've been living with you for the past month, Toby. I'm not scared of you." She hesitated after saying that as if she'd just realized the truth of that herself.

He needed to coddle her and reassure her he would never hurt her. Even if his heart and his brain were fighting over the right thing to do, he knew that to be true. Hell, he'd put himself in danger and gladly die if it meant her safety.

"And I have a boyfriend."

Something inside him snapped. All the

wavering he'd done on what was right or wrong and what he should do about her was now irrelevant. She was his. His! How dare she consider letting another man have her. "Yet here you are with me," he growled as he shot to his feet.

Her eyes got really big as she braced both hands on the couch beside her thighs. Her beautiful thighs she'd wrapped around his body nightly over the last month.

"Toby," she squeaked, but it was too late. He was too far gone.

He grabbed her, hauled her to her feet, spun her around, and pinned her to the wall. "C'mon, baby. You said you weren't scared of me."

"I-I'm not."

"You don't sound very convincing," he taunted. He leaned down and kissed her neck gently as he ground himself roughly against her. "If you love your boyfriend so much, why did you let me fuck you in every position? Take your virginity, for Christ's sake?"

"I, um, T-Toby, why are you doing this?"

He bit her shoulder hard, not enough to break the skin but enough to leave a mark of possession, and she cried out. "Because you're mine, and you've seemed to have forgotten that."

"No, I haven't," she panted. She squeezed his shoulders, but he wasn't sure if she was trying to push him away or pull him closer.

He pushed away from her and took several steps away. He pointed angrily at her. "Then don't fucking bring up that man again!"

He watched her swallow convulsively, and she finally nodded.

"You should leave," he gritted. He needed space before he did something he'd regret, like mate with her regardless of her boyfriend.

She shook her head. "I-I think we still have a lot to talk about."

He shut his eyes, running his hands through his hair. Adrenaline was still rushing through his veins at the thought of another man touching her, possessing her, and he felt as if no relief was coming. He was falling deeper into the abyss.

"If you stay, we won't be talking."

He pinned her with a stare, clenched his jaw, and fisted his hands at his side, all in an attempt to find some shred of control to cling to.

He watched her grasp the hem of her shirt, working it up, solidifying her decision, and reality seemed to have suddenly slowed.

"Krista," he said when he finally managed to find his voice. "I'm serious. You'd better be sure because I can't be gentle. Not now. Not when I have to think about you being with—" He cut off with a roar of frustration.

"Come here, Toby."

How she found the strength and conviction to order him like that he didn't know, but he wasn't in the right mind to figure it out either.

He started toward her and she backed away slowly, heading toward the alcove with the bed. He stalked her, enjoying the slow striptease she was giving him with each removal of her clothing. He followed her example and hastily removed his clothes. By the time they reached the bed they were both naked.

"You're fucking mine, Krista. You got that?"

She nodded as her legs finally hit the

side of the bed, but he didn't let her lie down. He grabbed her, spun her around, and pushed her front up against the wall, his chest melding with her back.

"Last warning," he purred into her ear. She rubbed her ass against his thick erection in response, and he groaned. "You little tease. I'm going to remind you just who you belong to."

He shoved his leg between hers and reached around the front of her. He slid his finger into her folds, finding her drenched in her honey. "You're wet for me. *Me,* Krista," he said into her ear as he grabbed his cock and entered her in one quick thrust. She gasped at the sudden intrusion, and he slid his other hand around to pinch and pluck at her nipples while he fingered her clit and pounded into her without pausing.

He fucked her hard, harder than he'd ever taken her, but he couldn't seem to ease up. He had to mark her, brand her. As he plowed into her, her hands scrabbled for purchase on the wooden walls, and her whimpering sounds forced him to take her even harder. Still fingering her relentlessly, he stopped torturing her nipples with his other hand and shoved it into her hair, grabbing it and forcing her to expose her neck. His fangs slid out, and he wanted to fucking take her, make her his for all eternity.

"Mine! You're fucking mine, Krista," he growled into her ear, shafting into her so hard and fast his balls were drawing up, a burning sensation igniting in his lower back, his stomach, his whole damn lower body.

She whimpered as her pussy started fisting around his cock.

"Say it! I wanna hear you say it."

"Yours," she cried out. "I'm yours, Toby."

He licked her neck, and she screamed as orgasm claimed her. Feeling her sweet little pussy grip his cock so painfully hard was his breaking point. He roared a totally animalistic feline sound as his balls drew up and he came in her, pumping until he was spent.

He slumped against her, exhausted, and tried to catch his breath, his muscles trembling from the adrenaline rush and the energy he'd just expended. Upon realizing he was probably crushing her, he eased back, and his cock slipped out.

"Shit," he breathed, seeing his seed trickle down her thigh. He'd taken her bare. He'd never done that before. Marking a woman on the inside like that was one way to make his mountain lion damn-near impossible to suppress. But that wasn't what caused the crushing mortification he suddenly felt as he watched the evidence of his taking.

Blood.

It was mixed with his semen. He'd taken her so hard he'd hurt her. All his musing about never wanting to cause her any harm didn't matter. He was a fraud. A dangerous, evil fraud.

"Jesus, I'm sorry." He wanted to rub her arms, comfort her, but he wasn't worthy of touching her.

She turned around and stared at him, dumbfounded. He took several more steps back and tripped over his feet to get away from her. He saw his robe out of the corner of his eye and grabbed it as he ran from the cabin.

He frantically thought back to their conversation. He'd given her an opportunity to leave. She'd said she wanted it. But was he too demanding? Too forceful? Oh God, what was the difference between that and rape?

He was going to be sick.

———

KRISTA HAD CRIED herself to sleep. Her conversation with Toby hadn't gone as planned. Nope, not at all. She'd decided to keep up with the boyfriend ruse, but when she'd reminded him of that, the look in his eyes almost made her come clean. He'd looked so devastated, so crushed. Then she'd seen the possessive need in his eyes. The need to assert himself as the alpha male in her life. She knew in that moment he always would be, and all the indecision regarding his little family secret suddenly seemed less important. She'd had a decision to make then and there. Either walk away or let him prove his dominance. She knew she had to walk away eventually, but she wasn't ready to live without him now, knowing when she did have to leave, he'd always have her heart. She loved him, and if she could've done anything to help him understand he was her only alpha, then she would've done it. She'd taken the first step by undressing and teasing him, lulling him, all the while easing herself into submission.

And he'd given her a mind-blowing orgasm with unbelievable sex. God, she'd never get used to the fireworks she felt when he touched her. And immediately afterward, she felt as if it'd worked, but then something changed. He'd panicked for some reason and left her alone.

She was left confused and upset that she'd made the wrong decision yet again. Nothing seemed to be going right, and to top it all off, she'd started her period.

After tossing and turning into the night while she'd cried—sheepishly putting some of the blame of her emotional state on it being that time of the month—she'd finally fallen into a restless sleep.

She wasn't sure how much later it was when she felt soft lips kissing her tear-streaked cheek.

"I'm so sorry, baby," she heard over and over as trembling hands circled her body. She tried to turn over and look at Toby, but his grip tightened. She felt his shoulders shake and his breath hitch as he kissed her hair. After several minutes he loosened his grip and started to ease away. "Oh, God, you probably don't want me touching you. I-I just wanted to make sure you were okay. I mean, I know you're not," he sniffled, "but I needed to man up and face what—"

She turned then, looking at his red eyes. What the hell was he talking about? "Toby, I'm fine, sweetheart."

"I had no right—"

She chuckled, and he looked at her incredulously. "I told you I wanted it."

"But I, er, hurt you." He looked down, not meeting her eyes.

"I am a little sore. I mean you're huge and all, but I'll live." She shrugged, not understanding where this was going.

"But you were bleeding."

Realization dawned on her. Had he thought he'd forced himself on her? She reached over and gently tugged his chin up, making him look at her. "I started my period, Toby."

His eyes got fractionally bigger for only a second or two, but then he gave her a sad smile and shrugged one shoulder. "Doesn't matter. I was way out of line. I'll leave you alone now. I-I just wanted to check on you."

She grabbed his arm as he started to get out of their bed—she'd thought of it as their bed for a while now. "I don't want you to go."

"I don't deserve to be near you right now. I don't deserve to be near you at all."

"Don't you think that should be left up to me to decide?" When he didn't respond, she sighed. "Please don't make me beg."

He shut his eyes, and the pained expression that crossed his face made her heart ache. "I'll do whatever you want," he whispered.

She pulled the covers to the side. "Take your clothes off and get in."

He stared at her for several seconds and then finally started to remove his clothing. In all the time they'd spent together, this was the first she'd ever seen his penis completely flaccid. She'd have her work cut out for her if she wanted to turn his mood around and reclaim the spark between them that had existed before today—or yesterday as it was now the early hours of a new day.

He climbed in beside her, not touching

her. She rolled over and tucked herself against him, but he didn't wrap his arms around her.

Oh, yeah, she'd definitely have her work cut out for her.

Toby still wasn't himself. Krista hadn't tried making love to him while she was on her period because even though she was new to the whole sex thing, the idea of that just grossed her out.

So, while she'd been on her period, she eased Toby back into some of their comfortable routine. He'd started holding her while they slept. He'd hugged her goodbye in the mornings before she set off to work in the office and he on the land. A few times she'd initiated a kiss, and he returned it because he knew it was what she wanted, but he'd immediately look away from her, too ashamed to maintain eye contact. No matter how many times she'd tried reassuring him that he'd only done what she wanted him to do, it never seemed to work.

A little voice in the back of her mind told her that maybe he was having such a hard time because he wanted to mate with her and knew he couldn't, that maybe he was fighting his animal side for control. She'd like to believe that because that'd mean he wanted her on an emotional level.

And yet he was barely touching her. She'd been off her period for days now with no sign of Toby moving their relationship back to the physical level it once was. She'd talked to Mikaela about this, and she'd first told Krista to be patient. But as the days passed, Mikaela was getting antsy on Krista's behalf and told her she should initiate sex with him.

Because he'd been treating her with kid gloves, she felt that uncertainty she'd felt in the beginning with him. Only this time, she didn't feel out of her element turning up the heat. With only two days left before her flight back to St. Louis, Krista had to tamp down her nerves and take back what she wanted.

After dinner at the main house, she and Toby returned to the cabin. They showered. Separately, with Krista showering first. When she got out and Toby got in, she made sure she put lotion all over her skin and sprayed on some light perfume. She slipped into bed naked, but that wasn't a big deal because they'd been sleeping in the buff. Not that Toby hadn't tried a few times coming to bed with pajama pants on, which she'd quickly grumbled about until he removed them.

When Toby came out of the bathroom, he had his wet hair combed and a towel wrapped firmly about his hips, gripping it in a death grip. Once he got to his side of the bed, he tossed it to the side chair and quickly got in, scooting close to her and casually resting his arm over her waist.

It was time to make her move.

She licked her lips, turning around to face him. "G'night," she murmured, pressing her lips gently to his. He stiffened —and not in the right place. But he tilted his head and returned the closed-mouth kiss. When he started to pull away, she leaned closer and nudged her parted lips against his mouth. He opened slightly, barely taking her top lip between his lips as she did the same with his bottom lip. When he tried breaking the kiss after the little smooch, she slid her tongue between his slightly parted lips and glided it over his tongue. He moaned softly as his hand rested on her hip.

But he barely kissed her back and didn't so much as move his hands from where they touched her.

Okay, so drastic times called for drastic measures. She ended the kiss and snuggled against him as if she were going to sleep, and he sighed contently as he did the same.

Then she kissed his chest, and the soft breathing that'd been coming from him stopped. She licked his nipple, then nipped the flat copper disk. He gasped, but stayed still. He had one arm under her head and the other wrapped around her back. When she started kissing a path down his abdomen, his arms locked around her, stilling her journey.

"What are you doing?" he whispered.

He might've stopped her descent, but he didn't incapacitate her completely. She bit his belly, then laved the mark as she turned her gaze up to meet his. "I'm going to suck your cock."

His swift intake of breath was confirmation she was on the right track. He wanted her, but he'd felt he didn't deserve her. Total nonsense. Toby was a good man. Krista understood he had a feral side, and she accepted it came with the total package that made up the man she loved. The fact that he'd been resisting her swelled her heart because *his* heart was in the right place even if his head wasn't.

His eyes searched hers, but when he didn't say anything or loosen his grip, she continued. "Do you not like it when I touch you like that?" She knew he did, but she needed him to confront his demons.

"I-I." He cleared his throat, shutting his eyes. "I love it," he breathed.

"Me, too." She went back to kissing his belly and tried to move lower, but his grip held her tightly in place. "Toby, I want this. You want this. Stop fighting it."

On a groan he relaxed only marginally, but it was enough to provide her the leeway she needed. She kissed and licked a path to his growing cock—not completely erect, but getting there. Her tongue slipped out and licked the dry head, and not only did his cock jerk, his whole body did. Within seconds he was fully engorged.

She ran her tongue down his shaft and gently tongued his balls. Toby was tense as he emitted small sounds and fisted the sheet. She smiled as she drew one of his balls into her mouth. Her lover was fighting it. Oh, she'd make sure he gave in. She was up to this challenge. She sucked his sac, drawing in the other, and Toby's already stiff thighs turned to steel.

She released his balls and licked up his shaft. Hmm, the head was no longer dry. He'd started leaking already. Toby might have been trying to fight his libido, but his body had different ideas. She sucked the plum-shaped head into her mouth, moaning as the salty taste of him landed on her tongue, and a deep guttural groan rumbled through Toby's chest.

Eager for more, she tongued the slit, trying to coax more out of him. God, she missed tasting him like this. It'd been too long since she'd had him in her mouth. She forgot about her seduction and lost herself in the man she loved. She engulfed him, sucking him to the root, and his hips shot off the bed. She sucked him hard as she reached down with one hand to play with his balls while using the other to stroke him with a rhythm that complemented her oral assault.

She didn't let up. She sucked, licked, and nipped at his cock as it throbbed in her mouth, and the sounds Toby was making were getting louder. As she bobbed on his cock, she felt his hand slip into her hair, and she felt a giddy thrill that he was finally allowing himself to enjoy what was happening. But as soon as his hand touched her head, it was gone, fisting into the sheet again.

As she worked his cock, Krista considered stopping before he came, forcing him to suffer or fuck her. But she immediately rejected that idea because knowing the Toby of late, he'd take the pain and suffering over pleasure. She quickly thought about her options as she slowed, settling on one that'd get him touching her and hopefully propel him into initiating sex. She moved, letting his cock slip from her mouth, but not straying away. She licked where his leg met his groin and nibbled gently. She heard Toby breathing heavy but felt his body relaxing a little. Did her lover boy think she was finished? Ha!

She shifted, moving her legs to the

other side of him as she licked along his shaft. Then she crawled, backing toward him and slinging her leg over his chest, putting her pussy just above his face. He snatched her thighs as his breath caught, but she took his cock back into her mouth and the breath he released was strangled.

She sucked him off, her hips undulating, enticing him to taste her. As she rocked above him, she'd worked her way closer to his mouth, his hot breath bathing her core. So close. God, she was so close to experiencing another orgasm from Toby's ministrations. She ached to feel him again.

She released his cock and dug her head into his thigh. "Please," she begged. "Please, Toby. I need you." She bit his rock-hard thigh, the sexual frustration becoming overwhelming. He hissed and bucked against her, his dick hitting her chin. She started to turn to bring him back into her mouth when she felt his hot, wet tongue on her outer lips. She gasped. "Yes."

His hands slid up her thighs and caressed her ass as he pulled her closer. When his tongue buried into her folds, they both groaned.

Krista took Toby's cock to the back of

her throat and swallowed against him like he'd taught her. He'd been such a patient and skillful lover during her time here, and she'd loved every minute of it. Even if he'd questioned it himself.

When she swallowed him, he gripped her ass tighter, spreading her cheeks and licking her everywhere. She was on a hair trigger, her orgasm building much faster than she'd anticipated. Oh, God, she couldn't come first. If she did, he might put a stop to this and not allow himself the same pleasure. She doubled her effort, jacking him off and sucking him with ruthless abandon. She felt him swell inside her mouth and his body tremble beneath hers. He moaned against her, and that sensation damn near sent her flying over the edge. At least he was close because she didn't know how much longer she'd last.

He bent his knees and thrust up as he started fucking her mouth while he stabbed his tongue into her pussy. He'd finally let go enough of his unfounded guilt to embrace her fully, if only physically—but it was a vast improvement. Her pussy clenched around his tongue, and he pulled it out and pushed a finger inside her. His lips surrounded her clit, and she knew she was a goner. With the first suck, she exploded, screaming around his cock as she sucked him hard and bucked against his face. The hand holding one of her ass cheeks held her still as he apparently lost himself in giving her pleasure, groaning as he ate her, drawing out her orgasm as long as he could.

In the back of Krista's mind she knew she'd feel defeated when she came down off this high because Toby hadn't come.

But just as that thought crossed her lust-hazy mind, his thrusts turned frantic just before his hips snapped up and stilled, a loud, agonized groan splitting the air as the first stream of his release shot down her throat.

She'd been coming down from her own orgasm as Toby reached his, but his taste and mindless ministrations propelled her into another one, her pussy clenching around two fingers now as she drank from him.

Some long moments later, she slumped against him and he went lax beneath her. He caressed her leg, kissing her inner thigh. Seizing the moment, she turned around to face him.

"Thank you," she whispered.

He rested his forehead against hers and held her close. "I'm sorry for everything. How I've been acting. For what happened that night—"

"Shhh." She shook her head, placing a finger over his lips. "Enough. I'm willing to agree to disagree on that if you'd just let it go. I don't want to spend the next two days living with this wall between us."

He sighed, nodding his head. "I just never expected to fall, er, feel this strongly for you. You deserve to be cherished and coddled, not manhandled." When she frowned at him he smiled. "Okay, okay. Letting it go now."

She smirked. "Good. Then I want you to do something for me."

"Name it," he murmured as he kissed her temple.

"Make love to me."

"Mmm, I think I can handle that." His lips traced a path to her mouth, taking it with a gentle, but thorough, kiss. And she opened for him, just as she knew she would always do. They kissed and held each other, exploring their mouths with their tongues, their bodies with their hands.

When Toby deepened the kiss, he rolled her beneath him, the weight of his body grounding her as her emotions soared. He settled between her legs and touched her everywhere he could reach as he kissed her jaw, her neck, her shoulder, her breasts.

When he was hard again and she was writhing beneath him, he pulled away and fumbled with the drawer of his nightstand. He pulled out a condom and rolled it on. Once he was prepared to take her, he kissed her briefly as he shifted into position. Then he pulled back and watched her eyes as his cock pressed into her. He clutched her hands, pulling them beside her head and twining their fingers together, all the while watching her eyes. He was making love to her so tenderly that Krista felt tears burn her eyes, but she quickly blinked them away. She didn't want him to misunderstand and stop.

They both groaned once he was fully seated within her, and he only hesitated a few seconds before he started fucking her with long, slow strokes. He pinned her with his heated gaze. They made love this way, watching each other, for what felt like hours, but she had no idea how much time had passed. Everything had blurred away except for the man holding her.

She'd never felt this close to him before, his feelings so raw in his eyes, and she was sure her emotions were clear to him, too. She wanted to tell him she loved him. It felt right, but she didn't want to chance ruining this perfect moment. She knew he had feelings for her—he all but confessed that just a while ago—but she also knew she was leaving him. No, she wouldn't tell him. She'd love him with her heart and her body, but keep the words to herself.

"You are so beautiful," he murmured. She groaned, shutting her eyes for the first time as his cock hit her sweet spot inside and raked over the little bundle of nerves. He did it again, and she gasped. "Open your eyes. I wanna watch you come. Please, baby."

She did, and he hit it again. She exploded around him, grabbing his shoulders and opening her mouth on a silent scream as she kept her eyes glued to his. He thrust a little faster, then stilled, groaning with his gaze still locked onto hers.

After they came, they held each other

and made love again, continuing the pattern several times throughout the night.

And Krista wondered how she'd ever find the strength to walk away from him.

———

OVER THE PAST TWO DAYS, Toby and Krista had been inseparable. Even during the workday. Mikaela had closed on the purchase of the Caldwell Tree Farm and didn't need Krista in the office. Toby's father and brothers understood his need to spend every second with Krista, so they hadn't pressured him into working either. Toby knew the clock was ticking, but he did his best to embrace Krista while he had her and not think the ugly thoughts about her boyfriend that'd instigated his rough taking of her a couple of weeks ago.

Happy thoughts. He'd tried to force himself to have only happy thoughts, putting most of his energy on creating pleasant memories with her to sustain him for the rest of his life. He'd remembered wondering if somehow Josh just knew Mikaela was his mate when he'd first been with her, and now Toby understood. His lion understood.

Krista was his mate; as unavailable as she was, she was still the only woman for him. He also got a new understanding of why his dad had never tried finding another woman after Toby's mother had died. It seemed so obvious to him now. Once one of their kind found his mate, that was it. There were no second chances with a runner-up.

Even though Toby had tried his best to be happy, no matter how strong of a front he'd put up, he still went through the emotions of grief because he was losing his one true love. He'd considered confessing his feelings and hoping she felt the same way for him, but then he knew he couldn't risk her life like that if she wavered with indecision. And he couldn't take the heartache if she reasserted her feelings for her boyfriend. So, while he'd enjoyed every moment with her externally, he'd grieved silently.

Now he was at the acceptance stage of his grief because there was no other choice but to accept what had to happen.

He stayed lost in his thoughts as he

helped Krista pack, and he felt numb, the pain deadening all feeling in his skin. Krista walked with him on each trip out to Mikaela's truck. She'd tried carrying some of her bags, but he begged her off, feigning a silly macho act he didn't really feel. When in reality he was dragging each second, stretching each minute with her.

With the last bag loaded, Josh stood by the driver side saying goodbye to his wife, and Toby stood around staring at Krista.

"I will never forget you," he whispered.

She blinked, her eyes tearing up, and he had to keep himself from grabbing his chest to assuage the ache there.

"Me, too."

"You touched my life, Krista. I—" *Shit*, he would not tell her he loved her. He would not do that to her. He took a deep breath and caressed her arms. "I'm going to miss you."

Her breath caught as a tear slid down her cheek. He reached up and brushed it away before leaning in and kissing her softly. She wrapped her arms around him, held him tightly, and he drank her in. One last time.

He ended the kiss and held her. He

wasn't sure how long they stood beside the big truck, but he finally willed his arms to let go, his legs to move back a few steps.

"Good-bye," she breathed as she opened the door. And he just couldn't say it back. Instead he brought his fingers up to his lips and kissed them before angling them in her direction and dropping his hands limply.

He watched them leave, keeping his eyes on Krista until he couldn't see her anymore. Then he'd watched the truck until it'd turned out of sight. Then he listened to the truck as it traveled down the road until he couldn't hear it anymore.

She was gone.

He looked up to see Josh watching him sympathetically. He couldn't take that. Not pity. Not right now. When his brother took a step toward him, Toby shook his head frantically as he backed away. Then he turned and shifted into his bestial side, running as fast and as far away as his feline legs would take him. He knew no one could see him.

But he had no misconceptions about the agonized roars tearing through his throat.

CHAPTER TWELVE

It had been almost two weeks since Krista returned home. Mikaela hadn't stayed, preferring to take a much-needed vacation. It was just as well. Krista worried that being so close to her friend right now would just be a reminder of what she'd lost.

After crying for several days, she'd turned stoic. Going through the motions of everyday life like some zombie and lying awake at night, just staring at the ceiling. When she allowed herself to think about her time with Toby, she realized she was a different person now. When she'd arrived on the Woods estate, she'd been a timid, sexually inexperienced lady. Now she was a woman, more secure in her skin. If only she'd allow herself the opportunity to embrace the change that being with Toby had ignited. But she wasn't ready yet. In time she would be, but right now she just couldn't go there.

It was late when she heard her phone ringing. Her heart raced as she jumped out of bed to grab it, but then she saw the caller ID, and her fragile hopes plummeted. Ariel. Not Toby. God, she missed him so much she ached. This was madness. She didn't have a boyfriend. She should be with the man she loved. Why was she not giving him a chance to be with her? Was it because she was scared of becoming a mountain lion like Mikaela?

When the phone wouldn't stop ringing, Krista finally answered. "Hello?"

"Hey, sis. Long time, no talk. I got your message and called you back, but I never heard from you. Everything okay?"

Hell, no! But she wouldn't burden her sister with the drama of her private life. If she could get Ariel to help Toby and his brothers break free from the prison of their estate, then her heartache would serve a healthy purpose. "I have a job for you. This is going to sound crazy, but just hear me out."

After getting her sister's promise to secrecy, Krista explained the Woods family secret, their dilemma caused by their urge to mate, and her theories about suppressing those instincts enough for them to socialize with society again.

Ariel listened with rapt fascination, asking excited questions whenever Krista paused long enough to take a breath. She'd have rolled her eyes if she'd been in a better mood. Her sister had always loved the unexplained and was more open to seemingly unexplainable phenomena than Krista had ever been.

"I just finished a project that was funded by a grant, so I'm actually free for an indefinite period. When can I meet everyone?"

"Er, um, how about next week?"

"I was thinking this weekend?"

"That's in two days!" Krista squeaked. But just as soon as she said the words, she felt a long-forgotten calm wash over her. She'd see Toby again. She wasn't letting Ariel do this on her own, even if her sister was a professional scientist. Okay, Krista knew the excuse was flimsy, but it was a lifeline to her. She cleared her throat. "I have to make some calls. If I can work it, how about Sunday?" At least that'd give her an extra day.

"Sunday's good. I'll see you then."

Krista hung up, her mind racing. She'd see Toby again by Sunday. It was three days away.

Too far away.

She paced, clutching her phone. The thought of what she wanted in life dominated all others. She'd always wanted to be an attorney, but since she'd returned from the Woods estate, that dream paled in comparison to the one she had about belonging to Toby forever. She could have both. Mikaela was a prime example. And she was happy.

Krista could be happy, too. As she thought about it, she felt her resolve settling in. She didn't know if Toby would have her after she lied about having a boyfriend, but she'd find a way to come clean without jeopardizing their lives. If she knew beyond a shadow of a doubt he wanted her above all others, she'd take that leap with him.

But she couldn't find out here. She had to go to him.

And Sunday was too damn long to

wait. Thinking well into the night, she decided she'd much rather inquire in person than make those calls on Ariel's behalf. And if she booked her flight now, she could be back on the Woods estate by lunchtime.

———

TOBY WALKED into the kitchen with his brothers during their lunch break on Friday. Their dad was interviewing prospective employees now that they had the adjacent Caldwell Tree Farm, so his brothers were excitedly talking about finally getting the help they needed.

But Toby didn't give a shit. Work was a distraction for him. It always would be since he had nothing else in his life. No woman. No wife. No mate. And he never would. It was a wonder how he was able to drag himself from his bed every morning. As he remembered those first few days without her, he knew he hadn't. It wasn't until the third day of drinking and passing out in his bed when his brothers rallied around him, forcing him to join the land of the living. So he got up, not always showering, and when he did, not always shaving—

like this morning—and worked, visited with his brothers, ran at night. But his heart wasn't in anything he did.

Because his heart was in St. Louis, encased in his beautiful mate, where it belonged.

He ate and joined the conversation when he was prompted to, staring into space when he wasn't.

"... meet in ten minutes." Toby looked over at Josh, who'd been speaking.

"What did you say?"

Josh sighed and gave Toby's shoulder a squeeze. "Mikaela had to run into town. She's on her way back and wants to meet with everyone in ten minutes."

"What about?" Jack asked, with the natural scowl on his face. Toby figured in time he'd be giving Jack a run for his money in the frowning department.

"She has some ideas about our mountain lion side. She didn't really elaborate, but she sounded excited about it when I spoke to her a few minutes ago."

The hum of the guys' voices drifted into the background as Toby went back to eating. This was just one more thing for his brothers to be excited about, and he wasn't in the right mind to join in the fun discussion about all the possibilities of what their sister-in-law was up to. He didn't care. It wasn't that he was an asshole about it. He just couldn't muster up the energy to be excited about anything.

After he finished eating, he walked to the back of the room to look out the window that overlooked their backyard. He stood there, staring at the thousands of trees in the vicinity but not really seeing them. It was her he saw. He didn't think of her name. He hadn't said it aloud since she left, and he didn't let it slip in his mind for fear he'd cry it out. But that didn't stop him from thinking about her.

Hell, he had no choice. And he wouldn't have it any other way. If he stopped thinking about her, he'd forget what she looked like, and that was unacceptable.

As he stared through the trees and into her beautiful eyes, he heard a door shut in the distance. A familiar smell assaulted his senses, and he almost buckled. It had to be the female scent of Mikaela reminding him of his mate, but that didn't make it any easier to accept. When he heard her walk and her voice in the kitchen talking, he turned to look at her.

The air locked in his lungs.

She wasn't alone.

She was with his mate.

All of his brothers shot their eyes to him and back to her before Josh cleared his throat.

"Hi, kitten. What's going on?" Josh asked his wife as he walked over and kissed her. "You said you had some ideas about our mountain lion sides."

Mikaela smiled, but Toby wasn't watching her. As soon as his eyes locked with his mate's he wasn't going to look away for fear she'd disappear.

"Actually, this was Krista's idea. After she learned our little secret, she mentioned her sister is a scientist and wondered if there was something that could be done to subdue the urge to mate with any available female." She looked over at the beautiful woman standing next to her. "Isn't that right, Krista?"

She cleared her throat. "Yeah." *Oh, God, her voice.*

"Krista," Toby breathed, unable to keep

it from slipping out of his mouth. She was really here, really talking.

She gave him a tentative smile. "Yeah, I called Ariel, my sister, when I was here, and she called me back last night. She understands the need for secrecy and is eager to meet with you all to see if she can help. She'll be here on Sunday if you agree." She was asking everyone, but she hadn't taken her eyes off Toby.

"Whatever you want, baby," he responded automatically. He'd give her whatever she wanted for the rest of his life.

"Wait, wait, wait," Jack said, rolling his eyes. "Just what the hell do you expect her to do?" Krista flinched, breaking eye contact with Toby and looking over at Jack.

Toby growled, shooting his gaze over to his overbearing brother. "Back off."

"No, no, it's okay, Toby. He has a right to understand this. You all do. I'm not sure what she's planning on doing because I'm not a scientist, chemist, and all those other things she is. I think she'll formulate some drug for you, but she's a professional. She won't just throw a bunch of dangerous stuff together and shove it down your throats. At this point, all I'm offering is the opportunity to see if she can help."

"Well, I think it's a hellacious idea!" Rob said, gleaming. "Is she single?" He wagged his eyebrows.

Krista smiled at Rob. "No, she's married to her high-school sweetheart."

"Well, damn." He rubbed his chin. "I still think she should come try her voodoo out on us. Couldn't hurt."

"Fine," Jack grumbled.

Mikaela clapped her hands. "Good. Then it's settled."

Nobody spoke for several seconds, the silence almost deafening. Toby was worried now that Krista had spoken her news, she'd be leaving. His skin felt tight as panic set in. His mate was here. He couldn't let her go. Oh, God, not yet. Please not yet.

"Josh, honey, can you call Jeffery and have him bring Krista's bags in? She'll be staying until her sister arrives on Sunday. He can put them in the second-floor guest room."

"No!" The word was out before Toby could stop it. He searched Krista's eyes. Were they sad because she didn't want to stay with him, or did she think he didn't want her staying here at all? He couldn't let her worry. "Have him take them to my cabin."

The relief that flashed in her eyes was almost his undoing. She still wanted him. No matter what their lives were like, she still wanted him. The joy that flooded him was damn-near overwhelming.

Mikaela turned to Krista for confirmation, and she gave his sister-in-law a quick nod. "Okay, then. Rob, Jack, I need to speak with you in my office. Honey, you can come, too," she said to her husband.

The people in the room slowly filtered out, but Toby was frozen in place. He wanted to yank Krista in his arms and never let her go, but he couldn't seem to move his feet.

"You look like hell," she whispered.

"I've felt like hell."

She nodded as she clasped her hands in front of her and twisted them nervously. "Can we, er, go back to your place and talk? I'd like a little privacy."

"Of course." He walked toward her, passing her to open the door for her, and led the way to his cabin in silence. He'd let her speak her mind before he said or did anything. Although he had no idea what he'd say or do given the opportunity. He was still reeling with the reality of her being here.

When they walked into his cabin, he winced. God, it reeked of booze in here. He quickly opened up the windows to get the air circulating and gathered the empty bottles while she sat down on the couch. He tossed the evidence of his weakness into the trash and turned to face her, resting on the wall for several seconds as he gathered his strength to sit next to her. When he finally couldn't stand the distance any longer, he took his seat and turned to her, their knees brushing against each other—it was the first physical contact he'd had with her since she'd left, and he immediately wanted more. So he rested his elbows on his knees and buried his head in his hands to stave off the urge to touch her just yet.

"How do you feel about me?"

His head shot up. How the hell was he supposed to answer that?

"I want the truth, Toby. No matter what it is."

"I love you." He said the words in a rush and felt relieved that they were finally free. "I love you," he said softer, slower, nodding his head to affirm the confession.

She reached over and took his hand. Her trembling fingers stroked his skin. "I love you, too."

He groaned, swooping in and kissing her heatedly. God, she loved him. His mate loved him. She kissed him back but pushed away after several seconds.

"I need to know if you can forgive me lying to you if I promise never to do it again."

"Baby, neither one of us is perfect." His heart was still racing with her words of love. "You can talk to me about anything."

She nodded and seemed to be bracing herself as she leveled a stare at him. "I'm not getting married."

Toby's brow furrowed as he looked at her. "So, you lied about getting married? That doesn't matter, baby. I understand if you wanted to protect your relationship with that man—"

"No, Toby. There is no man." His eyes got big as she continued speaking. "There's only you. Mikaela told me that I had to pretend to be involved with someone when I come out here to work. There never was a boyfriend."

"You're not taken?" He felt the words strain past his lips.

"No, sweetheart."

He jumped from the couch, roaring, his fangs descending. "Why didn't you tell me this over the phone? You need to leave right now." He stalked closer to her, fighting every step. He wouldn't hurt her again. He'd die before he let that happen.

"No."

He bellowed, grabbing his head and doubling over as he fought the pain, the need to take her, knowing that it was his love for her that bought him this measly time. If he hadn't been in love with her, he'd have already forced her into submission by now. He realized he was moving closer to her, so he looked up.

"Oh, fuck, Krista," he groaned. She was taking off her clothes.

"I love you, Toby. You love me. If you don't want me with you for the rest of our lives, you'd better say so right now." She pulled out some kind of dart gun. "I'll tranq you and leave. Your choice."

"You. Are. Not. Going. Anywhere," he gritted.

"Come to momma." She smirked as she tossed the gun aside, and he pounced.

There was no finesse. His clothes and the rest of her clothes were torn from their bodies. She clutched at his shoulders, trying to kiss him, but he wasn't having that.

"You will submit to me," he growled, flipping her around and shoving her onto her hands and knees on the floor.

"Oh, yes, Toby, take me. Make me yours."

He bit her neck, not breaking the skin, but to hold her in place as his cock thrust into her. He fucked her hard, not caring about any preliminaries. His mountain lion was in control right now, and it wanted to claim its mate. He'd play with her later. Right now this was about marking his woman, his lioness.

She moaned, wiggling her ass against him. He released her throat and pushed her shoulders to the floor. When she rested her head on the hardwood, her body completely open to him, he felt pride and love for his mate swell within his chest. She wanted him just like he wanted her.

Feeling his feral side relax, he eased out of her, turning her to sit astride him. She eased down on his cock, wrapped her arms around his neck, and buried her face in his hair as she rode him. He gripped her hips to help guide her and thrust up into her on each downward stroke she took.

His woman. His mate.

"God, I love you so much," he groaned, feeling his balls draw up as her pussy fluttered around him. She stroked one of his fangs and he snarled, but then she threw her head back and screamed as she fell over the precipice.

He roared as he starting coming, then sank his fangs into the smooth column of neck she'd exposed for him.

She whimpered as he held her tightly against him, but he couldn't let go. Not right now. Not while they were both coming. When her pussy stopped convulsing and his cock quit jerking inside her, he pulled away from her throat and licked the wounds, purring as he did so.

She giggled and squirmed against him.

"What's so funny?" he asked in an amused voice. He couldn't help it.

"That tickles."

"I'm grooming you, baby. Get used to it."

She gasped and pulled away. "Oh, my God! You *did* lick my hair the first night we met, didn't you?" Her look was a mixture of incredulity and humor.

He felt his cheeks burn. *Fuck*, he must be blushing. How embarrassing. "I, um, it's a natural—"

She shushed him as she kissed him lightly. "That's okay. You can lick me any-where you want."

"Good. Because I intend to lick you every day for the rest of our lives."

"Mmm... Sign me up for the licking. I can't wait to taste you all over again."

"I'm all yours, baby."

"Yes, Toby." She pulled back and stared into his eyes, gently rubbing his beard-roughened cheek. "Yes, you are."

EPILOGUE

Ariel Owens pulled up to the huge log cabin, excited to see if what her sister had told her was true.

Oh, she had no doubt her sister believed it to be true, but the idea of people turning into animals was so huge she needed to see it with her own eyes.

She got out of the truck and was immediately greeted by her sister and a damn fine-looking man. He was holding her hand. Interesting. Ariel never remembered seeing Krista date. She was always too busy burying her nose in some history, government, or law book. Not that Ariel hadn't been book-smart, too, but she didn't let her work life interfere with her private life. At least until last year.

"Hey, girl," Krista said, walking toward her. "This is Toby, my, um, fiancé."

Ariel gaped at her. *Wow. Good for her.* But if he was one of the mountain lion shifters...

"Are you two mated?" They both beamed like kids on Christmas morning. Ah, the honeymoon look. They didn't need to answer her question, it was written all over their silly smiling faces. "Never mind. I'll take that as a yes. But, um does that mean you're a mountain lion shifter, too?"

"Yeah. I didn't shift right away, though. We were too busy, er, getting reacquainted." Krista blushed, then fidgeted. "C'mon. I'll take you inside and introduce you to everyone."

Ariel followed her sister and this Toby dude inside the house and into a huge den. *Holy shit.* There were four more guys standing in here and three of them looked to be around Toby's age. They were all sexy as hell—even the older one had a little something going on. Had she fallen into some alternate universe with alpha male animal shifters with bodies to die for?

"This is Thomas Woods, Toby's father." Thomas stepped up and shook her hand.

"It's a pleasure, Mrs. Yates."

"Oh, no you don't. It's Ariel and don't you forget it, Thomas."

He smiled at her. "I think I'm going to like having you here."

"This is Toby's brother, Josh, and his mate, Mikaela."

"Nice to meet you two." They shook hands with her, returning the greeting.

"And these two over here are Jack and Rob, Toby's other brothers."

Those guys shook hands with her but watched her closely. She got a different vibe from them than she did the other two. Maybe it was because these two were unmated.

"So, Mrs., er, Ariel, what are your plans and when do you want to get started?" Thomas asked.

"Well, I want to start right now." She shrugged, looking at Jack and Rob. "I think there's been a misunderstanding. I'm not married anymore. How does that make you feel?"

There was a collective gasp in the air.

"What the hell are you talking about,

Ariel Michelle?" Krista admonished. "What about Will?"

"We grew out of love a long time ago and got tired of the pretense. Our divorce was final three months ago." She turned to the two brothers she'd addressed earlier. "I'm not involved with anyone either. I'm a totally and completely available woman. How does that make you feel?" she asked again.

"Shit, Ariel, are you lying?"

"My divorce papers are in my briefcase. You can call Will if you want. He's vacationing in Italy with his new girlfriend, though."

"Fuck, get her out of here!" Josh yelled right as Rob and Jack shifted into snarling mountain lions.

Ariel smiled. They were real. No fucking way. This was going to be the highlight of her career.

———

ARIEL OWENS IS a biochemical engineer who trusts science above all else. When her sister claims her new boyfriend can turn into a mountain lion, she thinks the poor woman has finally lost her marbles. Her sister insists she needs her help, dangling the possibility of a major discovery right in front of her. How can she resist something like that? She'll humor her and play along, but if she's going to do this, it'll have to be done her way or not at all, in **Surrounded by Temptation**, the next book in the Woods Family Series.

LIKE YOUR HOT alpha men with a side of danger? The Bang Shift Series contains full-length, contemporary romantic suspense novels, featuring mercenaries, mechanics, and the mafia! Start this hot, wild ride with **Brody**, the first book in the Bang Shift Series. FREE on all retailers!

HEY, y'all!

Thank you for reading my book. :) If you enjoyed it, I'd be very grateful for a review. If you didn't like it, then share that, too... as long as your review is honest, that's all that matters.

And ice cream. Ice cream matters, too.

Want the latest scoop? Be sure to sign up for my Newsletter! I mean, it's not as yummy as ice cream, but nothing ever is.

Xoxo,
Mandy

Surrounded by Temptation

Surrounded by Secrets

Young Adult written as M.W. Muse

Goddess Legacy

Goddess Secret

Goddess Sacrifice

Goddess Revenge

Goddess Bared

Goddess Bound

 Mandy Harbin is a *USA Today* Bestselling author who loves creating stories that explore the complexities of everyday relationships...with some kissing thrown in. She is a Superstar Award recipient, Reader's Crown and Passionate Plume finalist, and has achieved Night Owl Reviews Top Pick distinction many times. She also writes young adult romance as M.W. Muse because teens like kissing, too.

After graduating college and working many years in technology, she threw caution to the wind and began studying writing at the UALR. Years of trashed manuscripts and rejections eventually led to contracts and representation. With over thirty books published, she now serves on the board of her local writing chapter.

Mandy lives in a small, Arkansas town with her husband and their bossy dog, enjoying her own happily ever after...with some kissing thrown in.

www.mandyharbin.com